WESTERN SHORT STORY SHOWCASE

VOLUME ONE

JOHNNY GUNN   L.J. MARTIN   JOHN NESBITT

V.J. ROSE   GARY MCCARTHY   VONN MCKEE

WOLFPACK
PUBLISHING
— EST 2013 —

Western Short Story Showcase

Big Sam and Salazar by Johnny Gunn
The Way of the West by L.J. Martin
Trail's End by John Nesbitt
The Infamous Bandit Queens by Gary McCarthy
The Gunfighter's Gift by Vonn McKee
A Promise Broken, A Promise Kept by V.J. Rose

Paperback Edition
© Copyright 2018 (as revised) Various Authors

Wolfpack Publishing
6032 Wheat Penny Avenue
Las Vegas, NV 89122

ISBN: 978-1-64119-366-5

WESTERN SHORT STORY SHOWCASE

PART ONE

BIG SAM AND SALAZAR BY JOHNNY GUNN

Big Sam and Salazar

Johnny Gunn

Copyright 2018, Johnny Gunn

Wolfpack Publishing
6032 Wheat Penny Avenue
Las Vegas, NV 89122

BIG SAM AND SALAZAR

"DAWN'S EARLY LIGHT, MY ACHIN' back," he said to himself, buckling the cinch on old Rusty. He hitched up his trousers fastened the bat wings, and swung into the saddle for another long day chousing cows out of the high country for the fall move to winter pasture. Then the sky lightened some, all the colors, reds, yellows, blues, oranges, all of them, burst through the granite gloom of night, and once again Derek Sam knew why he was a range riding buckaroo of the old school.

"Try this on for size, city boy," he muttered, kicking Trusty Rusty into a gentle lope, taking him up a long grassy draw toward heavy brush, big trees, and rocks the size of barns. It was just a minute or two and Jesus Salazar reined in alongside. "Buenos Diaz, Teo," he called.

"Good morning, Derek," Salazar answered back. "Do you remember where we saw that little bunch late yesterday. Find them again, and it will take the rest of the day to get them down to the pens."

Derek Sam is half Paiute and half Irish and Jesus Salazar is half Mexican and half Irish, and the two have been riding together for years, drinking together for years, celebrating the life of the buckaroo for years. "See you're riding Rusty. Looking for some rough country today, eh?" They started their circle in a strong trot, and as the country began to steepen, slowed to a good walk. "What was that slop cookie tried to shove at us this morning?"

"Teo, listen here. If I had to analyze ever stinkin' thing that fool fed us, I know for a fact I would die of hunger. Couldn't make the day, though without some of his hard tack. He calls them biscuits, but what they are, for sure now, are young rocks ain't growed up yet."

They started working their way through the heavy brush, aspen trees, some pine, and still lots of good grass on the ground. "Think that bunch should be over that ridge, there," Sam said, pointing to a spot about half a mile to their left, and slightly uphill. "Why don't you go on up high, I'll top the ridge and wait for you to start them. Work on their right, and I'll take the left, and let's see if we can make a nice line for them to foller.

"Get a leader to start a line and the rest'll just tuck right in." Moving cows along a fence line is one thing, moving them through brush and timber is another. But cows like to play follow the leader, and if you get the right one to be leader, some of your work is done. "This bunch looks like mostly yearlings, Teo. Hope we get an old and wise cow to stand for leader." Getting a bunch of animals that have been in the mountains for months without contact with big old men on big old horses to do what you want them to do takes a lot of patience and knowledge. "Nice and slow, now, Teo. Let's just ease 'em down. Wish we could tell them there was fresh alfalfa at the pens, but with all this good grass up here, they might just tell us to go to that other place."

Both men got very quiet for the next couple of hours as they moved the cows into what might be considered a rather small herd. Slow and easy, no rodeo crap on the range, horses that have been responsible for moving thousands of head of cattle, buckaroos that grew up in the saddle, and a knowledge of what they had to do, all worked their magic, and some fifty head moved off the mountain.

One problem with cattle is they aren't always as trail wise as the men and horses trying to get them somewhere. A steer will bolt for no reason at all, and the buckaroo has to get him back into the herd without losing any others in the process. It takes a very cow wise horse to work as partner with the man in the saddle, and both Sam and Salazar had exceptional mounts. Two or three times one particular steer bolted, and two or three times one or the other of the men brought him back.

"Tricky little devil, isn't he?" Sam said on the last episode. They continued down the long slope to the corrals and pens where trucks were waiting to haul the critters to the home ranch about twenty five miles away. As they moved down, they picked up a few strays and it wasn't long they were trailing a full herd of steers and cows. "Would you look at the size of that big old boy?" Sam said as Salazar eased an old mountain wise steer into the herd.

"Probably five years old, and we're probably the first men he's seen in four of them. Keep your eye on him real close Teo, he could be trouble." The old ones that go for years evading capture are wise and dangerous. They become the herd leader fast, and can mess up a trail drive instantly. "If he takes off, just keep the rest of the herd together, Teo. Letting him go won't affect anything else."

It was a hassle for another couple of hours, keeping, what the men were now calling "bullhead" in line was hard. First on one side, then on the other, he would bolt, and take some young ones with him. It would be a chore to capture the young ones and get them back in line. "It looks like Mr. Bullhead has a plan, Sam. He's a steer but he wants to be a bull. It looks like he wants to scatter this herd and make it his." He spoke his mind just as the steer made his play, stomping the ground, tearing up the grass, snorting like a real bull, and trying to run off a dozen or more steers and cows.

"Work our herd, to hell with him," Sam yelled, spurring Rusty into action, watching Salazar do the same thing. They moved fast to head off the yearlings and cows, and get them back into the herd, which was beginning to separate into little knots of fives and sixes. Just as Rusty turned the lead yearling, Bullhead charged, driving his head and well over a ton of old beef into the horse's flank. All three, Bullhead, Rusty, and Sam went down in a heap, and Derek Sam was beat from top of his head to bottom of his feet as two massive animals tried to regain their feet.

A well trained cow horse will stand when his rider dismounts, whether by choice or otherwise, and Rusty got to his feet and stood next to Sam's now quiet body. Salazar had the steers back in the herd and rode quickly to the wreck. "Sam," he hollered, jumping from his horse and running to where his partner lay. "Sam, are you alive?" For just a minute, there was no answer, no movement. Then a groan, and Salazar knelt next to his friend.

"I'm hurt bad, Teo. Leave Rusty with me and take

the herd down. We're only a couple of miles from the pens, and get me some help. I ain't gonna die on you partner, so don't be goin' through my duffle when you get down there," and he tried to chuckle but it just hurt too much."

"I was looking forward to that, too," Salazar gave it right back to him.

"I got busted things everywhere, Teo, but if I just stay quiet here for a spell, I might be able to get back on old Trusty Rusty. Get going now, we sure as hell don't want to miss cookie's fine offering tonight, now do we," and he groaned again, trying to get somewhat comfortable.

Salazar pulled Sam's long coat from the back of Rusty's saddle and covered his friend, stepped into the saddle of his cow pony and started toward the herd that was beginning to scatter some. "Get back as quick as I can, amigo," and loped off to finish the job.

"If I'd a moved you, Sam, you'd be dead right now. Arms and legs and ribs all askew. If you were bleedin' it was inside. I didn't see any blood, 'cept of course on your head where you tried to break that rock." Teo Salazar had got most of the herd down, lost a few year-lings but they could be picked up easy the next day.

They brought a couple of good pack mules, made a litter, and moved Sam down where an ambulance could pick him up and drive him some fifty miles to the nearest city, Elko, Nevada.

Sam spent several days in intensive care, and the one man that was there every day to make him better was his trail partner, Jesus Salazar.

"Take a while for that leg to get fixed, though. Boss said you better be ready to move the herd to summer pasture come spring, so you'll have a good winter. I'm gonna be cow boss until you're back on your feet. Don't fall off any more horses, OK?

"Oh, hey, I almost forgot. They fired Miss Rosario and moved cookie from range camp to home ranch. You'll get to spend the whole winter eating those biscuits you like so much," and the laughter rang down the hallways at the Elko general hospital.

A LOOK AT: NAME'S CORCORAN, TERRENCE CORCORAN: A TERRENCE CORCORAN WESTERN

BY JOHNNY GUNN

Terrence Corcoran carried a badge in Virginia City, Nevada until one day, in a drunken stupor, he shot the sheriff. Now he's returning to the Comstock looking to get his badge back and stumbles into a conspiracy that might put the sheriff, district attorney, and others in jail for a long time. A lovely working girl is brutally murdered, a Hungarian duke wants a Wells Fargo gold shipment, and the sheriff rehires him after first kicking him in a most tender spot. Corcoran was born on the ship bringing his family to this country, ran away to the frontier at an early age and brings his ideas of the old country and knowledge learned of the west to whatever mess he finds himself in. He's carried a badge, found himself in jail, and stands four-square for right, honor, and truth. You gotta love the guy.

AVAILABLE NOW ON AMAZON

ABOUT THE AUTHOR

Reno, Nevada novelist, Johnny Gunn, is retired from a long career in journalism. He has worked in print, broadcast, and Internet, including a stint as publisher and editor of the Virginia City Legend. These days, Gunn spends most of his time writing novel length fiction, concentrating on the western genre. Or, you can find him down by the Truckee River with a fly rod in hand.

Gunn and his wife, Patty, live on a small hobby farm about twenty miles north of Reno, sharing space with a couple of horses, some meat rabbits, a flock of chickens, and one crazy goat.

PART TWO

THE WAY OF THE WEST
BY L.J. MARTIN

The Way of the West
L.J. Martin

Copyright 2015 L. J. Martin (as revised)

Wolfpack Publishing
6032 Wheat Penny Avenue
Las Vegas, NV 89122

eBook ISBN: 978-1-62918-316-9

THE WAY OF THE WEST

"AYE, Mr. Hogart, I hear you perfectly well, and I understand you, but I still think it's about as good an idea as ticklin' a mule's heel to cure your toothache." Big John Newcomber spat a stream of tobacco juice in the dust to punctuate his point.

"Come on inside and let's gnaw a cup of coffee," Hogart said, trying his best to sound like the men who worked for him.

The owner of the recently renamed Bar H, Harold L. Hogart, reared back in his chair, stuffed his fat banker's cigar in his mouth, and narrowed his eyes. He wasn't a banker, but he was the next thing to it; he was an investor. And he had invested in the Bar H a year ago after old man Well's lost it to the Merchant's and Farmer's Bank—but then, old man Well's wasn't the only one to lose a ranch in 1886. All hoped this year would be a lot better.

The two men took a seat at the plank table that served the bunkhouse. And Hogart did his best to sound the empire builder. "You and I have gotten along fine so far, Newcomber, I hope to continue the relationship...But you've got to abide by my wishes, and his mother and I wish to have our son accompany you on this drive."

"I've already got a half dozen whelps green as gourds, Mr. Hogart—"

"Then another won't matter much. Wilbur will be ready and waiting at sun up. He's eighteen, older than some of your hands, and perfectly capable. We want him to have this experience before he leaves for college in the East."

So it was settled. John Newcomber had his back up over the whole affair, but he said nothing knowing from long experience as a *segundo*, foreman, that it was hard to put a foot in a shut mouth, and besides, it's usually your own throat you slice with a sharp tongue —and he wasn't about to walk away from a good job when even a poor one was nigh impossible to find. Still and all if he could change the man's mind, he'd give it a go, but he knew that trying to make a point when Hogart thought otherwise was like trying to measure water with a sieve. He'd end up all wet with nothing to show for it. Hogart was slick as calf slobber, but he was the boss.

Ah Choo, the cook, who was nicknamed Sneezy for obvious reasons, filled the two men's coffee cups, but was thinking of his honorable ancestors as he did so —which he had a tendency to do when he had to face unpleasant tasks. He was the bunkhouse cook at the Bar H, not the main house cook. That was Mrs. O'Malior's job. The two of them spatted like a pair of cat's whose tails had been tied together before they were tossed over a clothesline. And this afternoon, Sneezy had to go to the main house to round out his chuck for the month-long trip ahead. He did not look forward to the afternoon's chore, nor to having John Newcomber, who he had to be as close to for the next month as a tick in a lamb's tail, start on a long drive with a burr already festerin' under his saddle.

Mr. Hogart finished the varnish Sneezy called coffee, acted as if he enjoyed it, then rose and extended his hand to Newcomber. "You know how important this trip is to the Bar H, John. These cattle have to be in Mojave by the 16th of September in order to fulfill the contract with Harley Brother's Packing. A day late and those robber barons will want to renegotiate, and the price I have now will just barely cover this year's costs. Be there on time."

"God willin' and the creek don't rise...and some

tenderfoot don't stampede the stock, we'll make it. Dry year or no." He couldn't help put the dig in to the boss's withers like a cocklebur, but it rolled off Hogart like rain off an oiled slicker, not that there'd been enough rain this year to test the theory.

Hogart left the bunkhouse, and John Newcomber stood at a window staring out through the dirty glass, shaking his head. "This is gonna be like startin' a long trip with a sore backed horse and hole in yer boot sole," he mumbled, more to himself than to Sneezy.

"Pardon, Mr. Maycom'er?" the little cook asked.

"Nothin', Sneezy. Pack a lot o' lineament and bandages, an' a Bible if you own one. I got a bad feelin' about this go."

"Yes, sir, Mr. Maycom'er, sir. Renament and ban'ages and the Christian book, snap snap."

Morning dawned fresh and breezy, with the Sierra's at the ranch's back and the Whites, also the better part of 14,000 feet above sea level, between it and the rising sun—it took a while before the sun touched the Owen's Valley bottom with its warmth. It was the better part of two hundred fifty miles down the valley and across a piece of the Mojave Desert to reach the rail station at Mojave, and to be comfortable they'd have to average ten miles a day to keep the schedule. Ten miles should be easy, all things being equal. But John Newcomber had driven stock long enough to know that all things never stayed equal for long.

Sneezy had rung the chuck bell at 3:30 A.M., a half hour earlier than usual, so he could feed the men the last of the eggs and milk they'd see for a good while, and still get a jump on the herd. He wanted to stay ahead of them if he could, at least on this first day—for he'd be eating dust the rest of the drive. And the four-up of mules he had pulling the chuckwagon would keep ahead of the herd, given no major trouble.

True to his father's word, just as Sneezy whipped up the chuckwagon team to get a jump on the drovers, Wilbur Hogart pranced up on one of the Hogart's blooded thoroughbreds, a dun colored horse with fine long bones that stood sixteen hands. It was a pleasurable animal to look at, but... He carried a quirt and wore a fine new Palo Alto fawn colored hat, twill pants, a starched city shirt, and English riding boots—on his hip gleamed a new Smith and Wesson chrome plated .38 in a polished black holster. The bedroll he had tied behind the saddle couldn't have carried more than one blanket and one change of clothes. John Newcomber stood cinching up his sorrel quarter horse as Wilbur's animal proudly single-stepped over to the hitching rail.

"John," the young man said, "I'm ready—"

"You'll call me Mr. Newcomber while you're working for me," the Bar H *segundo* said quietly, his

voice matching the cold-granite of his chiseled face—
but Wilbur heard him clearly enough. The young
man's eyes and nostrils flared a little, but he said
nothing in reply. "Understood?" Newcomber asked,
unsatisfied with the boy's silence, his own voice a trifle
louder.

"As you wish, Mr. Newcomber," the boy replied,
stressing the mister in a manner that rang of sarcasm.
John left it at that, knowing it would be a long trip and
that time and the trail would work out most of Wilbur
Hogart's kinks. Hard work had a way of doing that to a
man, or breaking him, if he wasn't much of one to start
with. John really had no way of knowing if Wilbur
Hogart had any sand, but time and the trail would tell.

"Dad said I was to ride point," Wilbur added,
rubbing salt in the spot Harold H. Hogart had already
galled on John's back.

"You'll ride drag, like all new hands do, Mr. Hogart." John Newcomber swung up in the saddle, forking
the sorrel and waiting for him to kick up his heels with
the first saddle pressure of the morning—he didn't, but
John knew the sorrel was saving it for later. He took
the time to switch his attention and give Wilbur a
hard look.

The boy glared at him. "Dad said—"

"Wilbur, let's get something straight right up front.
Your daddy's not going on this trip, and if I hear you

say one more time, 'daddy said,' I'll not take kindly to it and I might lose my temper. I've got a deep well of temper, Wilbur, and I can lose it every hour of every day and not run out. It's been tested. That's the kind of trip this might be, Wilbur, if you say 'daddy said' ever agin'."

"But—"

"There ain't no butts about it, Wilbur."

"Yes, sir," Wilbur said, to his credit, and reined the tall dun colored horse away.

Sally Fishbine had ridden for the Bar H for fourteen years, the first thirteen when it was the Lazy Loop, and the last one under John Newcomber. He reined his bandy legged gray over beside John and paced him out to what they called the creek pasture, where the eight hundred fifty-seven head, by yesterday's count, of Hereford mix—with Mexican Brahma— were gathered. The rest of the hands, a dozen of them, were holding the cattle and getting their minds right for the drive.

"Salvatore," John said quietly as they gigged the horses toward the creek pasture, "is the weather a'gonna hold."

"Bones say it is," he said, stretching. About that time John's sorrel decided he was awake enough to shake loose, and began a bone-jarring humpbacked dance. "Step lively!" John shouted, giving the big horse his spurs and whipping him across the ears with the rein tails at the same time. The sorrel settled, and John knew from long experience that that was it for the rest of the day.

"I swear, you two are like an old married couple...got to have yer spat or you can't get the blood to pumpin'," Sally said, rolling a smoke with one hand as his own mount plodded along.

"Both of us got to show how young we still are," John said, reaching forward and patting the big horse on the neck. "If'n I didn't pop 'is ears ever' morning, he'd think I didn't care for 'im."

They picked the pace up to a cantor, with Wilbur Hogart keeping a respectful twenty paces behind. Wilbur had learned to ride English, in Oakland at the Hogart's breeding ranch, across the bay from their home in San Francisco, and he could sit a saddle with the best of them by the time he was sixteen, and rode jumpers, but it was different from western riding—considerably different in that you handed the horse to a groom when finished for the day, and you finished for the day whenever you tired of the animal and the exercise. Still, he knew he was equal to anything the country and John Newcomber could throw at him—at least he was quite sure he was.

They crested a rise and looked down into creek canyon, and a thousand bald faced and mixed breed cattle lowed and grazed while a dozen cowhands waited the chance to earn their dollar a day and found.

Stub Jefferson had ridden in the year before, and John Newcomber had hired him on without so much as a second glance. His rig, and the way the black cowboy sat the saddle and kept his own council was enough of a resume for John.

Sergio and Hector Sanchez, a pair of young brothers up from San Diego were hired on just for the drive. John knew nothing about them, other than they rode fine stock and carried the woven leather reatas of the vaquero, and theirs were well tallowed and stretched to seventy feet with the weight of many a cow.

Old Tuck Holland had been working cattle on the east side of the Sierra for as long as John could remember. He had tales both older and taller than the Sierra's and would tell 'em until they chopped ice in Death Valley, if you'd listen. His age was indeterminable but he had to be on the shady side of seventy. He looked so puny he'd have to lean against a post to spit to keep from blowing himself down; but he was tough as wang leather, had a face carved and etched like a peach pit by sun, sand, and wind, and spent most of his time looking back to see if the younger hands were keepin' up. And they were struggling along wondering why he made it all look so plum easy.

Colorado, which was the only name he gave and consequently was the only name used for him, was red-headed befittin' his name, bow legged enough that a pig could charge twixt his knees while he was clickin' his heels, and loud; but he pulled his own weight. He too had been hired on just for the duration of the drive.

Pudgy Dickerson was the last of the hands hired on, and John had to bail him out of the Bishop jail in order to do so, but he needed a hand and the rest of the able bodied men in the valley had run off to another silver strike in the high country—another whiff of bull dung as far as John Newcomber was concerned. But particularly when times were tough men seemed to jump at the chance for easy money. It normally turned out to be grit and grime and beans and backache, but still they chased the will o' the wisp.

The remuda man was Enrico Torres, as good a man with horses as John had ever seen. He pushed three dozen head of rank half-broke stock so the cowhands could trade off a couple of times a day. It was hard country between the north end of the Owen's Valley and Mojave. Some spots of good grass and sweet water, but more than enough hard-as-the-hubs-of-hell ancient lava flows and flash floods, cactus and snakes, and heat if the weather decided it wanted to run late, or snow if it ran early. And it usually decided to do one or the other—and sometimes both—when a herd was being shoved to market. It was hard on horses and men, and hard as hell on a good attitude...

They pushed the herd out, jittery, but then all of them were when a drive began and before they settled into the routine. The men found their positions, all unassigned except for Stub Jefferson, the black cowhand who was riding point, and the Sanchez brothers, who were assigned drag with Wilbur Hogart and quickly took up positions flanking and staying out of the dust. The Sanchez boys had ridden enough drag to know they could stay out of the most of it on the flanks, and still do their job. So they gave Wilbur the position of honor...or so they told him...dead center trailing the herd.

John Newcomber floated from position to position, judging the men he didn't know, watching the herd, eyeballing the weather, and worrying—that was his job.

They hadn't gone three miles before Wilbur Hogart let his horse drift over close enough to Hector Sanchez so he could call out to him. "I'm Wil Hogart," he called.

Hector looked over and nodded, and touched the brim of his sweat soiled sombrero.

"What's a fella to do about the privy?" he shouted again.

Hector looked at him, a little confused.

"I need to pee," Wilbur said.

"Sí," Hector repeated, "the señor needs to 'pee.'" He reined over closer to the fancy looking gringo, who didn't look quite so fancy now that he was covered with a half-inch of dust. "Well, señor, you ride sidesaddle to accomplish that task."

"Sidesaddle?" Wilbur questioned. "You're funnin' me, *amigo*. I meant do you take the drag while I drop out, or just what?"

"Señor Newcomber will be very angry if you stop to water the sagebrush, señor. It is the tried and trusted sidesaddle method—"

"Fill in for me, señor," Wilbur said, and reined away to find a bush, which was no problem as the country was chaparral covered.

"Sidesaddle," Hector said to himself, then laughed aloud. He couldn't wait to tell his brother.

"Sidesaddle," Wilbur repeated to himself, pleased that he had not fallen for the obvious prank of the other rider. He knew he would be the butt of many attempts, but was wise to them.

He dismounted and unbuttoned his trousers and began to relieve himself, just as the grass under his attacking stream came alive in the most terrible buzzing and thrashing Wilbur had ever heard. He stumbled back and pawed at the Smith and Wesson when he realized it was a four-foot rattler he had the misfortune to awaken from his repose in the sun.

Wilbur emptied the six shooter, managing to scare the snake into retreating even faster than he already was, but not managing to kill it.

Still, Wilbur was satisfied with himself—until he heard the men begin to yell, and felt the vibration of four thousand hooves begin to beat in rhythmic stampede.

"My God," Wilbur said aloud to himself. "Did I...?"

He raced for the thoroughbred, mounted, and rode after the advancing wave of cattle and men, and into a wall of dust as he had never seen.

The cattle ran for three miles, then the heat and the sun dissuaded them and they slowed, and finally, no longer hearing the explosions that had set them off, stilled and grazed.

John Newcomber sent Stub and Sally back along the flanks to pick up any strays, and checked with each of his men to make sure they were present and accounted for.

Wilbur Hogart, who sat at the rear of the herd, catching his breath as the thoroughbred stood and hung his head sucking in wind, was the last man he approached.

"You managed to keep from getting ground up," Newcomber greeted him.

"Yes, sir."

"Let me see that firearm," Newcomber said, his face turning to granite.

"It was a snake, Mr. Newco—"

"You shot at some poor ol' snake who was trying his best to get the hell out of the way!"

"He was only a couple of feet away, makin' a terrible noise."

"Give me that weapon."

"Dad said—"

"What did I tell you about that 'dad said." Newcomber snapped.

Wilbur looked red faced, but quieted and reached down and slipped the Smith and Wesson out of its holster and handed it over. Newcomber slipped it into his saddlebag. He eyed the boy up and down shaking his head. "Don't make any more trouble, Wilbur. You just cost the Bar H about a thousand dollars in lost weight. At a dollar and a half a day, not that you're worth that, it'd take you some time to pay it back should Mr. Hogart want his due."

"A thousand dollars?"

"A thousand dollars...that is if we get all the steers back."

John reined the sorrel away.

Wilbur sat chewing on that for a while, when Stub and Sally approached, pushing a half dozen head that had strayed during the stampede. They reined over next to him as the strays rejoined the herd, kicking up their heels like a reunion of old friends.

"You the *jefe's* pup?" Sally asked.

Wil gigged his horse over and extended his hand. "I'm Wil Hogart." Sally shook with him, but Stub just touched his hat brim, and Wil said "Howdy."

"Did the boss tell you about Oscar?" Sally asked.

"Oscar?" Wilbur said.

"Oscar, the new hand with the six kids and the crippled wife."

"He didn't say—"

"Oscar got stomped under." Sally said, keeping a straight face. Stub eyed him but, as always, kept his own council.

"Stomped under?" Wilbur asked.

"Ain't enough of 'im left to bury," Sally said, shaking his head sadly.

"You mean—"

"Oscar's cold as a mother-in-law's kiss, boy." Sally looked as if he was about to break into tears.

"It's all my fault," Wilbur said, his face fallen.

"Don't know about that," Sally said. "It's the Lord's place to judge reckless behavior...the kind what causes the good to die young. Yer misbegotten ways will be laid out a'fore St. Peter soon enough. You may not even survive this drive. Many won't. Maybe you'll meet Oscar in heaven and can explain to him why you got him stomped into salsa. Well, it's nice to make yer acquaintance." He reined away. Both he and Stub were doing their best not to break into uproarious laughter, and in doing so, their shoulders quaked. Wilbur thought they were both in the throes of grief.

"Aren't we going to bury him?" Wilbur called after them.

Stub turned back, wiping the tears of laughter from his eyes. "He's already stomped so deep he'll take root and sprout." He turned away, and the shoulders shook again.

Wilbur Hogart had never felt so terrible. What kind of a man was John Newcomber to worry about running off a thousand dollars worth of fat, and not even mention a man who had been stomped to death?

The word traveled quickly among the men, and all stayed away from Wilbur for the rest of the afternoon— knowing they would break into laughter if they rode up beside the dejected boy, and give it away. Wilbur clomped along behind the herd, his eyes and ears filled with dust, his mind filled with remorse.

They caught up with where Sneezy had made camp, an agreed spot ten miles from the home place on the edge of Bar H property and on the bank of a fair cold creek, lined with willows, a couple of spreading sycamores, and a few Jeffery pines.

Wilbur was the last to the camp, and the men parted from a group as he rode in—Wilbur presumed it was because he was approaching, and that they didn't want to have anything to do with the man who'd caused Oscar's death. Not that he knew who Oscar was. He'd only met a couple of the men, and Oscar had not been one of them.

Wilbur dropped the saddle from the thoroughbred and turned him out with the remuda, then walked straight over to John Newcomber.

"They told me about Oscar," he said, his weight shifting from foot to foot. "I want to go back and pick up his body. A Christian—"

John Newcomber gave him a dubious look and started to say something, but was interrupted.

Sally stood nearby and offered quickly, "Oscar wanted the coyotes and other critters to have him, boy." Sally removed his hat and placed it across his heart. "It was his last wish. He always was a kind soul to the little critters. And it's the way of the west. We'll say a few words about him after we bean up."

Wilbur was still unsatisfied, but didn't know what to say. It was a custom he'd never heard off, but little would surprise him with what he knew of cattle drives and drovers.

"The coyotes?" he finally managed to mumble in amazement. His gaze wandered from man to man, but none would meet his and none offered to disagree with what he thought was a pagan practice.

"Oscar was a religious soul, but he was the outdoors type...thought these here mountains was his...what do ya call them fancy churches... his cathedral. He wanted to be spread all over these mountains," Sally added. "Nothing like a band of the Lord's scavengers to spread a body about. Crows and buzzards and such fly for miles doing their business and the coyotes and skunks and wolves'll deposit him in all the places he loved—not in exactly the way I'd personally favor it, but he'll get spread. Ashes to ashes, dirt to dirt, dung to dung, so to speak."

Wilbur thought he was going to be sick to his stomach. All the men turned away, and some were obviously overtaken with grief. They held hands to face and shook, or turned away. He walked away from the camp and into a clump of river willows and found a rock by the creek and sat, watching the water tumble by, wondering what would happen to "Oscar's" six starving children. He sat there until he heard Sneezy bang the bottom of an iron skillet, and hurried to get his beans—grief and remorse was one thing, hunger was another.

The men ate in relative silence. Once in a while,

one would mention one or another of Oscar's children, or his crippled wife.

The men cleaned up the biscuits, bacon, and beans, and hauled their tins to Sneezy. Darkness was creeping over the camp, and chill setting in. The drive would take them from 5,500 feet elevation on the slopes of the Sierra that rose to 14,000 feet behind them, down to less than 2,000 feet at the railroad corrals at the town of Mojave.

"Time for the ceremony," Sally said. "Gather round, boys."

All the men gathered in a circle, standing, drinking their coffee, gnawin' chaw, smoking roll-your-owns. "Now, what do you remember about Oscar?" Sally said. "You start, Stub."

Stub removed his hat and scratched his woolly head. "Well, I ain't much on reminiscence, so to speak, but I might remember something, given as how Oscar was such a fine fella." He took a long draw on the tin cup then began. "You know that ol' Oscar used to run the Rocking W down near San Berdo. He was countin' cattle there for a buyer from San Francisco, and knew the W didn't have enough cattle to meet the contract, so ol' Oscar set his countin' chute up again' a small hill. The buyer set up on the top rail and went to markin' off the stock. Ol' Oscar had the boys drive those heifers and steers round and round that hill till

35

the buyer counted what he needed, then drove the herd off to the yards. The W got paid for nigh 500 hundred head...twice. Oscar saved the Rocking W, which the bank was sure to grab."

The boys laughed at that, but Wilbur found it to be downright dishonest. He smiled tightly.

"How 'bout you, Tuck," Sally encouraged the old cowhand.

"Well, Oscar was a tough ol' bird." Tuck scratched his wrinkled chin and its stubble of a day's growth of beard. "One time the foreman of the Three Rivers Ranch bet him a season's pay that he couldn't make love to an Indian squaw, kill a grizzly bear, and drink a fifth of whisky in one day...and the foreman knew where the bear's den was and knew an ol' squaw who was a mite friendly to all the Three River's hands, were they to bring her a bag o' beans or sugar. Well Oscar took that bet, but the thing was, he drank the fifth a' rye first, then...a little confused with the fire water an' all...he shot the ol' squaw dead as a stone. The hard part was holdin' that griz down...but he did an' that's why some bears here a'bout is such sons a' bitches."

The boys laughed and slapped their thighs.

Wilbur began to get a little suspicious.

"How about you, Colorado?" Sally asked the pock-faced redheaded cowhand. He sat away from the others, sharpening a ten-inch knife on an Arkansas whet stone.

"I never much cared about tellin' tales," he said, and spit a mouthful of tobacco juice, then went back to his work on the blade.

"You, Pudgy," Sally asked the man John Newcomber had bailed out of the Bishop jail to join the drive.

"Nobody," Pudgy began, "could ever find his way home, good as old Oscar. One time over at the Whisky Holler' saloon in Virginia City, old Oscar went up to the bar with a bunch of hands he'd just finished a drive with, and they got to drinkin' and drinkin'. A couple of the boys, realizing how drunk ol' Oscar was, went out to his nag and turned the saddle around—they didn't want him riding into trouble. Oscar, hanging onto that poor ol' nags tail, rode clean to Sacramento before he sobered up and realized he was facing backward. He never could find his way to Sacramento after that, unless he reversed his saddle. But he was always real good at knowin' where he'd been."

By this time Wilbur was red in the face.

"We need to cheer up," Hector Sanchez said, after he quit holding his sides from laughing. "A little friendly competition. Who's the newest hombre to sign on?" Hector asked.

"Must be ol' snake killer," Sally said, putting an arm around Wilbur's shoulders. "You get to go first."

"Wait a minute," Wilbur said. "Did any of you fellas even know this Oscar fella? In fact, was there even any Oscar at all?"

"I've knowed a few Oscar's in my day," Sally said. "How about you, Stub."

"Cain't say as how I ever knowed an Oscar."

All the men broke into laughter, slapping their thighs. Wilbur reddened again, and he felt the heat on the back of his neck. He didn't know whether to get angry and stomp away or offer to fight, so he just stood and got a silly grin on his face.

"Ain't you proud you didn't cause nobody to get hurt with that fool stunt?" Sally said, more serious than not.

Tuck cut in before Wilbur could answer. "Give the boy a chance to show he's as good as the rest a' ya," old Tuck looked serious. "Ya'll been funnin' him enough."

Hector stepped over in front of Wilbur. "Can you swing an ax, Señor Hogart?"

"I imagine."

"Good, then we have the notch cutting contest."

"Notch cutting?"

"Sure, every drive has the notch cuttin' contest."

John Newcomber walked away shaking his head,

but was unseen by Wilbur who was anxious to redeem himself for being stupid enough to be taken in with the stomped in rider story.

"Notch cutting," Hector said. "You go first, so the rest of us know what we have to beat."

Sneezy had already fetched the double bladed ax out of the chuckwagon and offered it to Hector. "Come on, over here," he led Wilbur to a fallen log, two foot in diameter.

"This is a good log for notch cutting," Hector said, and the other men agreed with him. He lined Wilbur up in front of the log. "Get your distance, *amigo*," he suggested, and Hector adjusted his distance from the log.

"Now, here is the rub, *amigo*." Hector stepped behind Wilbur and encircled his head with his red checkered bandanna.

"Hold on, now," Wilbur tried to protest.

"This is how it is done, *amigo*. Blindfolded. You can do it."

Wilbur allowed himself to have the blindfold put on.

"Wait until I give the signal," Hector said. "Your hat, *amigo*," he said, and removed Wilbur's new fawn colored, now dusty, wide brimmed hat. "You will do better without the hat."

"One, two, three, go," Hector called and, and the men yelled their encouragement.

Wilbur with vigor born of embarrassment and a desire to show these men he was equal to any of them, swung the ax five times before Hector yelled for him to stop. "Time is up, *amigo*."

Wilbur reached up and removed the blindfold, anxious to see how much of a notch he'd cut. And he'd cut three fine ones...in his hat. His new Palo Alto lay in front of the log, it's crown split, its brim with two wide splits.

"*Carumba*," Hector said, a sorrowful look on his face, "you have cut the notch right where I put your *sombrero* for safe keeping."

The men roared with laughter.

"You win the contest, Wilber," Tuck said. "The prize is a free millinery re-design. That's now what's known as an Owen's Valley special."

Wilbur's mother had bought him that hat, just for this trip. The anger began to crawl up Wilbur's backbone, and to the men's surprise, he cast the ax aside and went after Hector Sanchez with his fists. Hector was quick as a snake, and back peddled as Wilbur took four or five healthy swings, then charged in low and tackled him and drove him to his back. He got astride him and pinned him down. Wilbur was red in the face and spitin' mad, but he couldn't move.

"Hey, *amigo*, you can't take a joke?" Hector asked.

"Let me up and I'll show you."

"I think I hold you here a while until the pot she don't boil so much," Hector said.

"Let him up," John Newcomber said, crossing the clearing from where he'd been leaning against a log, taking it all in. "And Mr. Hogart, you will find your bed roll and a place to bed down. The fun is over."

"You might think it's fun."

"I notched my hat, as did most every man here. It'll pass and you'll see the humor in it."

"The hell I will."

Hector unloaded off of him, and Wilbur regained his feet, spun on his heel and stomped away.

"Remember the Alamo," he said under his breath, but no one heard.

He found a spot away from the others for his bedroll, and ignored the feigned compliments to his hat the next morning as the men ate beans and cornbread by the dawning light. He turned in his tin and got a handful of jerky and hard biscuits for his noon meal, and was the first to saddle up for the day's work.

The wrangler, Enrico Torres, cut out a new horse for him—ignoring Wilbur's suggestions that he ride his own thoroughbred with a terse, "Horse has to last the trip, and you will get a new *cabillo* at least twice a day, sometimes thrice, from here on."

The ragged looking buckskin selected by Torres stood and allowed the curry comb then the saddle and bridle, but went into a stiff legged bounce as soon as Wilbur forked him. As much as the boy fought to control the animal, he turned and bounced right through the middle of Sneezy's camp, kicking fire, and ash, and dust in every direction. The Chinese cook scattered for cover, cursing in Oriental jabber, then sailed a pot lid after the boy and high-jumping horse as they moved on into the chaparral.

But to the surprise of all who watched in amusement, Wilbur stuck in the saddle.

He tipped his hat after he got control of the animal, yelled, "Sorry Sneezy," then gigged away the snorting horse, keeping the animal's chin pulled to its chest, to take up his position riding drag.

"Not bad for a stall-fed tenderfoot," Enrico said to Sally and Stub, who were currying their animals near-by. "His ridin' ability is a bit better than his sense of humor."

"Spent his first day admiring his shadow, 'cause there was no mirror handy," Stub said, "I thought at first he might be studyin' to be a half-wit, but I believe he might just end this trip knowin' dung from wild honey. He's game enough, and has more sand than I figgered."

"I dunno," Sally offered. "He seems to me he's

taken too much of a liking to thick tablecloths and thin soup, but we'll see...we will see. My bones is goin' to achin', weather's a' comin'."

Before noon, the sky turned from deep bright blue to flat pewter and the temperature plunged forty degrees. The wind whipped down out of the Sierra, and men pulled coats from rolls behind their saddles.

Wilbur Hogart had a coat, but a light one that served as little more than a windbreaker, and the gloves he pulled from his saddlebag were kid leather—not working gloves, nor warm. Before long, he was cold to the bone, hunkered over like a ninety-year-old man, and shivering in the saddle. To add injury to insult, the hole in the crown of his hat leaked water, and his head was soaked.

Hector Sanchez had kept his distance and the two young men had no more than exchanged glances.

By mid-morning, flakes of snow began to drift. Both Enrico and Hector Sanchez had pulled heavy *serapes* from the rolls at the back of their saddles, and their wide sombreros kept the snow from their shoulders. A steer began to fade back from a position between Hector and Wilbur, and both men moved to haze it back into the herd.

As they did so, Hector spoke for the first time that day. "You do not have a heavy coat?"

"I'm not cold," Wilbur managed through teeth gritted to keep them from chattering.

"I see that, *amigo*," Hector said, and smiled and reined away.

"Greaser," Wilbur said under his breath, and pulled the light jacket closer as he moved back to his position. At least the dust had stopped.

After a moment, Hector again moved closer and yelled to Wilbur. "I must leave for a *momentito*. Cover the flank."

Wilbur said nothing, even though he heard. He watched the Mexican gig his horse and lope away, then laughed to himself. If the herd did fade and stray on Hector's side, Hector would get a dressing down from Newcomber. He ignored the herd on Hector's flank and tended only those cattle directly ahead of him.

But as fate and the cold would have it, the herd did not stray but rather bunched closer, and Hector soon returned. He drifted over to Wilbur and tossed him a bundle. "It was Oscar's *serape*." He laughed and slapped his thighs. "He needs it no longer so he left it to me. It is not because I am generous *amigo*. If you continue to knock your teeth together like the castanets, you will cause another stampede. And more work for us all."

Wilbur held the wool *serape* in his hands and stared at the young Mexican, saying nothing.

"Ayee! You stick your *cabaza*...your head through the slit, tenderfeets."

"Though the slit," Wilbur repeated. And without hesitation, learned the use of the *serape*. The same one he had seen Hector use as a blanket the night before.

"*Sí, amigo,*" Hector said, and spun his horse to return to his position.

"*Gracias, amigo,*" Wilbur called after him.

"*Da nada*, Wil," Hector said, and gave the spurs to his horse. "You have mastered the *serape*, a difficult task. Tomorrow, if the weather is better, I will teach you the use of the reata...it should be nothing for a man who can chop a notch as you can."

"Tomorrow, if the weather is better," Wil called after him, and wondered what new trick Hector had up his sleeve and he knew that if Hector was fresh out, the others weren't. He wondered if he could borrow a needle and thread from Sneezy to sew up his hat—if Sneezy wasn't still wanting to sail pot lids at him for riding through the middle of camp.

But he was sure Sneezy had long forgotten the incident.

The wind picked up again. But he didn't care. He was warm, for the first time that day.

He removed his hat, eyed it skeptically, and began to chuckle.

A LOOK AT: NEMESIS (THE NEMESIS SERIES BOOK 1)

BY L.J. MARTIN

The fools killed his family...then made him a lawman. This wild and wooly western, in the Louis L'amore tradition, comes from renowned author L. J. Martin, whose over 20 novels have brought compelling reading to so many. McBain, broken and beaten from the Civil war, is reluctant to return to his family, as a snake dwells in his belly and he can't get the images out of his mind...until he learns his sister and her family have been murdered. Then it's retribution time.

AVAILABLE NOW ON AMAZON

ABOUT THE AUTHOR

L. J. Martin is the author of over three dozen works of both fiction and non-fiction from Bantam, Avon, Pinnacle and his own Wolfpack Publishing. He lives in, and loves, Montana with his wife, NYT bestselling romantic suspense author Kat Martin. He's been a horse wrangler, cook as both avocation and vocation, volunteer firefighter, real estate broker, general contractor, appraiser, disaster evaluator for FEMA, and traveled a good part of the world, some in his own ketch. A hunter, fisherman, photographer, cook, father and grandfather, he's been car and plane wrecked, visited a number of jusgados and a road camp, and survived cancer twice. He carries a bail-enforcement, bounty hunter, shield. He knows about what he writes about, and tries to write about what he knows.

PART THREE

TRAIL'S END BY JOHN NESBITT

Trails End: A Western Short Story

John D. Nesbitt

© Copyright 2018 (as revised) John D. Nesbitt

Wolfpack Publishing
6032 Wheat Penny Avenue
Las Vegas, NV 89122

TRAILS END: A WESTERN SHORT STORY

THE SUN overhead looked as if it hadn't moved for two hours. It just hung there, hot enough to melt hell's hinges. My horse was still walking, but it had been a day and a half since we'd had water, and his eyes were starting to roll. I said, half to myself and half to my horse, "We'll be gettin' to water soon. It's not time to stand in line for a harp yet." I knew that on the other side of those buttes there was a little dirty town known as Five Pigs, and even though it didn't have much, it had water.

Dusting down the main drag of Five Pigs, looking slanchways out from under my hat brim, I saw towns-folk lounging in the doorways. They didn't like my looks, I could tell, but they didn't have no corner on that market. And I couldn't say as I blamed them. At the horse trough in front of the livery stable I let my horse drink about a gallon or so, then pulled him back so's he wouldn't waterlog himself. After I tied him to the hitching rail, I plunged my own head into the trough. It felt good. Pivoting on my heel, I picked my sombie off the saddle horn, loosed the thong on my Colt, and headed for the watering hole known, according to the shingle that passed for a sign, as the Silver Gila. A sawed-off little jasper no cleaner than myself, leaning against the wall of the general store, spoke up.

"You ought not to be so stingy with your hoss on a hot day like today, stranger."

By now my mouth was wet enough to afford the luxury of a spit, so I did. Not at him, but into the dust off the side of the sidewalk. "Was I you," I said, "I'd mind my own. If I want any talk out of you, I'll slap it out." I raked him with a scowl that I thought might keep him for a while, then clunked along the board sidewalk and pushed myself through the batwings of the Silver Gila.

"Whatcha need, stranger?" the barkeep asked, as he polished a glass with what he must have called an apron. Looked to me like he was getting the glass greasier as he went along.

"Three fingers Red-Eye," I said.

I took in the crowd in the saloon as I tossed down the whiskey. This was a hard-case bunch, I could tell that. The drought wasn't making any of them any richer, and if I ever saw the fear of sheep in cattlemen's faces, I saw it then. Not that they took me for a sheep-herder, but maybe for a sheep man's hired gun. I wasn't anybody's hired gun, but I thought these fellas might want to push me around, one way or the other. I decided to keep them on the run before they tried to buffalo me.

I cleared my throat and shot an oyster into the spit-toon. "Barkeep!"

"Yeah, what now?"

"More whiskey!"

With his left hand, he skidded the full bottle down the bar to me. "Just remember to pay before you pass out," he said. He kept his right hand below the bar—on a double-barreled Greener, I figured.

"Barkeep!" I put more bite into it this time.

"What the hell you want now?"

"Two of your cigars." With his left hand, he pulled two out of his shirt pocket and tossed them on the bar.

"Need a match?" he sneered.

"Nope, just company." By now I had picked out the guy I figured was the town's Billy Bad-Ass. He was standing hipshot at the bar, wearing a tall Stetson pushed back and a Colt tied way down on his leg. "You," I said, "shag your ass over here and have a drink and a smoke with me."

His hand hung right over the grip of his Colt. "Yeah," he said, "and who might I be obliged to for such hospitality?"

"Deke Maginnis," I said, and that did it. The chatter stopped dead, the poker chips quit rattling, and everybody froze. "Don't let a name scare you," I said. I bit off the end of one cigar, spit it onto the sawdust floor, licked the cigar, and lit it. By now the big galoot had joined me.

"Sorry I didn't recognize you, Mr. Maginnis," he said. "Of course, I'll have a drink and a smoke with you, and be obliged."

"That's good," I said, curling my lip at the rest of the crowd. "A man likes a little sociable company after he's crossed over the country I just crossed. Never seed so many dead steers in one year."

"And it's a damn bloody shame," he said. He dropped a shot of whiskey into his neck, and set his jaw grim. "These damn woolly lovers have sheeped us off the upper range, and now they're crowding us off the waterholes. Next thing you know, there won't be such a thing as free range in this territory. The way the cattle are ganted up and dropping off like flies, it'll be a wonder if any of the little ranchers make it through this year."

"The hell you say," I said, taking the crowd at a glance. I picked up a quarter and tossed it at a peach-faced lad barely big enough to fill up a Stetson. "Here, Sonny," I said, "you go out to the hitching rail in front of the livery stable, and you take my steeldust gelding, and you let him drink about a gallon and a half or maybe two gallons of water, and you tie him back up. Anyone puts in his two bits worth, you tell him to send the bill to Deke Maginnis."

"Yes, sir," he chirped back, and hustled out through the batwings.

"And you," I said to my new *compadre*, "what's your handle?"

"I'm Niles Nelson," he said, "and mighty pleased to make your acquaintance, Mr. Maginnis. Seems to me you might be the best thing that's happened to this town in a while." He looked around to the other ranchers in the crowd, and they all grumbled yeah's and I-think-so's and you-betcha's. I took the lead from there.

"If you don't mind my saying so, Mr. Nelson, the whole lot of you look like you've looked at your hole card and it wasn't pretty."

"I don't mind a man speaking the truth, Mr. Maginnis. The fact is, these four-flushin' sheepherders have got us with our backs to the wall."

"Yeah," broke in another, "they got us between a rock and a hard spot." The crowd in back started grumbling again.

"Well," said I, and they quieted, "it looked to me, as I came across this country on the way in, that they've done sheeped out the upper grassland along the Little Sisters range, and they're takin' over the Gila Flats. Next thing, they'll have you pushed up against Buitre Pass, and on the other side of that there's nothing but broken country, all rocks and sand, with no more grass than a jackrabbit could live on."

"You hit it dead center, Mister," said one grizzled old coot.

"Well," I said, "seems to me you fellas got to get organized. You can't let those sheep lovers run roughshod over you and ruin the range. Come a good year, and good rain, this range'll be fit for grazin' again, 'less you let them over-graze it."

Nelson took over again. "That's just what we've been talkin' about, Mr. Maginnis. And what we need is someone to pull us together. Someone to ramrod us so we can push back!"

"You look like a man cut out for it," I said dryly.

"Me, no sir. I can hit a silver dollar at fifty paces, and I can fork my own broncs, but I'm no leader. We need a leader, someone we can look up to—someone that'll strike fear into the hearts of those stinkin' sheep-tenders."

At this point the whole saloon was rumbling with yeah, you betcha, you damn right, and so forth. I thought to myself, they think I'm the Texas Gun. I dropped another shot down my gullet, winced, and regarded Nelson narrowly. "What's your bargain, Nelson? I know you're not just talkin' to pass the time of day. Let's palaver."

"I think I speak for the Cattlemen's Association of Five Pigs," he said, looking around to the crowd. They all muttered that he did. "We'd like to offer you ten percent of each of our herds, come fall roundup, in return for your getting us back our waterholes and our range."

"That sounds mighty temptin'," I said, "but I got no hankerin' to go out and shoot a bunch of sheep. Next thing you know, you got to shoot a few sheepherders, and then someone's got to bury 'em. Don't know as that's my line of work."

"Mr. Maginnis," Nelson resumed, "you do the work you see fit to do, and the rest of us will look after the cleaning up. Ten percent?" He stuck out his hand, and I shook it.

Next day, the Silver Gila was fuller than before, and I'd guess every rancher in the territory—exceptin' sheepmen—was at the meeting. When everybody had wet his whistle, and got his sap flowin' I banged on the bar with my hogleg and called the meeting to order.

"You gents," I hollered out, "have asked me to take the lead, and I've agreed to do it. But I have to know, before I take another step, if I have your complete support."

There was a long and loud rumble of damn-betcha and hell-yes.

"And I want you to know that we can't pull this thing through without personal sacrifice on the part of each and every one of you. And I don't mean lives. Every one of us can come through this fight alive, if we move right. But you're gonna have to be willin' to give up a little of what you've worked so hard to earn."

"We've already done that by offering you ten percent," one ranny shouted out.

"I'm talkin' about more than that," I said, "and not for me, neither. I mean sacrifice." That held them for a minute, and I rolled a quirly and lit it. I shot out a cloud of smoke, then addressed them again. "You men still with me?"

There was a louder rumble than ever before. These men wanted to stop the tide of sheep.

"All right. Each of you go back to your spread and sit tight until you hear from me. Stay away from lighted windows, and don't ride the range except you go two or three strong. And don't shoot no sheep until the party starts. You'll be hearin' from me. Meetin's adjourned."

Nelson came up to me as the cattlemen dispersed, and he poured me a drink. "By the lord Harry," he said, "I think we've got more group spirit than we've ever had before. What do you have figured for your first move, Mr. Maginnis?"

"Tomorrow, come good daylight, you and me, Mr. Nelson, we ride."

THE SUN WAS BURNING the nipples of the Little Sisters when Nelson and I rattled our hocks out of Five Pigs the next morning.

"Your canteen full?" I asked.

"You bet."

"Your Winchester loaded?"

"Yep."

"Good. You might need both before this day's through."

"I know you've got a plan, Mr. Maginnis, but could you give me an idea what it is?"

"My think-box don't work like most men's," I said.

"That's why we wanted you," he said, quickly.

"This here's a plan that some men won't like."

"You're the leader."

"You remember what I said yesterday about sacrifice?"

"Sure, I do."

"Well, today's the day we jump into it, with both boots."

First ranch we rode into was the Vaca Flaca. We

reined up and called out to the owner, one Ben Whitley. He came bowleggin' out of the ranchhouse like the whorehouse was caught on fire. "Well, Maginnis," he said, "are we ready to move?"

"Yep," I said, "and we start right here. Whitley, I want you or one of your hands to set fire to your house and barn and sheds, and pull over your windmill, and then all of you ride with us."

"What?! Burn my headquarters?"

"It's either burn your headquarters or lose your hindquarters," I said. "If we want to stop those sheep, we got to burn off the range so they won't have anything to push forward to."

"What about my cattle? What will they do for feed and water?"

"When we get those stinkin' sheepherders pushed back over the other side of the Little Sisters, you'll have good grass and water, and plenty of it."

"I sure hope you know what you're doing!"

"You voted for me, didn't you?"

"Yeah, I did."

By noontime the range was covered by a thick black smoke as the withered grass went skyward in a million wisps. By then we had burned a dozen ranch headquarters, and we were over sixty strong. The range we rode over was hotter than a blacksmith's apron, and every man jack of us had a handkerchief tied over his nose and mouth to keep out the black particles that filled the air. Nelson pulled his cayuse alongside mine as we headed for the biggest ranch, the Rolling Willow. "Maginnis," he shouted, "how much of this we got left to do?"

"We gotta burn the whole range," I hollered back, "the whole length of Gila Flat, to keep them from coming any farther."

"Then what?"

"Then we start pushing."

"Back across the Little Sisters?"

"That's the only way." I spurred my horse onward, to see if we could get out of this cloud of smoke and catch a breather at the Rolling Willow before we set a torch to it.

I knew that Jack Kenton, the barrel-chested, two-fisted owner of the Rolling Willow, would not like what I had in store. He met us at the gate, Winchester in the crook of his arm. "What the hell you men think you're up to?"

"We're fightin' fire with fire," I said, leaning with both hands on the pommel of my saddle. "We're burning a swath of no-man's land between the sheep and the rest of this valley. It's the only way to stop them at this point, to give them nothing to push ahead for."

"What do you think you're gonna do here?"

"Think, hell," I snorted, "I know. Just what we did

at the other places. These men," I said, with a sweep of the arm, "have made their sacrifice, and they're here to see that you make yours." He took one look at the rest of them, every one of them grimy with soot, sweaty from hard riding, and grim-set from their work.

"All right," he said, "but let me get a few things out of my ranch house."

"Make it quick," I said, "we're traveling light." Two punchers rode forward and roped the support posts of his windmill, and a couple more started setting fire to his hayloft. These men were taking to their work with enthusiasm. Smoke was billowing out of the barn when Kenton came rushing out of his house, stuffing deeds and portraits into a flour sack. "Now we ride," I commanded, and we were off again, stronger by a dozen men.

Back in Five Pigs, the town itself was filmed in a light coat of ash. The hitching racks were lined with cow ponies standing hipshot. The saloons were filled— there couldn't have been a cowpoke on the range. What cows hadn't been caught in the grassfire had been pushed up against Buitre Pass, with no water and feed. The ranchers had gathered in Five Pigs to wait for my next move.

In the Silver Gila, I commanded a poker table and a bottle of Red-Eye. I hadn't had to pay for a drink since my first one in this town, and I was getting to like it. I put my spurred and booted foot up on the poker table, and I slugged down a shot of whiskey.

"Boys," I said to the men within hearing distance— and the sidewalk was crowded outside as well— "Boys, we struck a mighty good blow today. I'd say we drew first blood. And I'm proud of each and every one of you for putting the common good before your personal needs and wants. Each of you has done his part in stopping that dirty grey blanket of sheep from coming any farther. Come sundown tomorrow, we'll have pushed those smelly woollies on t'other side of the Little Sisters. Then we push the cattle back across the burned range to the grass and water on Gila Flat. This basin will be ours again, and any snivelin' sheepman will think twice before he crosses the Little Sisters again. For right now," I said, hoisting my drink aloft, "we drink to the campaign!"

The silence broke and a rumble followed. These men had gambled, and the winners' stakes were now within their grasp. I could tell they knew it, what with the scattered oaths and curses that rippled through the crowd. Any sheepmen who were around come sunup would be in a bad way, after all that these cowmen had lost.

I was just putting my other foot up on the poker table when a long-legged hombre pushed his way through the batwings and up to the bar. He looked familiar, but I couldn't place him. "What the hell kind of barbecue you men having in this country, anyways?" he asked, clinking his coin.

He being a stranger, no one answered. It was up to me, I guessed.

"Laredo," I called out to the barkeep (that was his name, I'd learned), "give this man a cigar. Come over here and have a drink, stranger, and tell me what you rode through today, and from where."

He downed a shot of my whiskey and wiped his upper lip with his lower. "I come over from Cinco Piedras today, through the Little Sisters." That quieted the crowd, for we all wanted to know how the sheep-herders had taken in the burn job we'd done.

"Well," I said, "here's how." And I tipped back my drink, and then filled us both up again. "Tell me, stranger, how did them oily woolly-chasers seem to be actin'?"

"Oh, I met them t'other side of the Little Sisters. They didn't seem to be too worried, just glad to get back over on t'other side."

"We scared them that quick, eh?"

"Don't reckon they were that scared."

"What you mean by that?"

"Seems they'd sheeped out all the grass on Gila Flat, and dried up the water holes, to where they couldn't have kept but a few hundred head of sheep anyway, so they pulled their freight yesterday. Said the cows could have what was left. They'd come back next year. Me, not caring all that much for woollies, but not looking for any more trouble than naturally came my way, I just pushed on. They were right about the grass and water—Gila Flat's about as smooth and dry as a lizard's belly."

The saloon was quiet as a morgue, and everyone was looking at me. "The hell you say." The words came quickly to me.

"The hell I do say. And by the way, what was all the burnin' down here in the valley?"

"You ask a lot of questions for a man who hasn't even told us who he is," I said, not exactly pleased by the turn things had taken.

"Name's Deke Maginnis, if it's anything to you," he said. He poured himself a whiskey with his left hand, keeping his right to linger above his pistol butt. "What's yours?" He smiled like he knew the answer, and my hole card never looked poorer than it did at that moment. He bit off the end of his cigar, licked it, and lit it, while he waited for an answer.

Nelson broke the silence. "See here, stranger, this man here is Deke Maginnis, as he himself told us, and just today he led us on a campaign to burn out those scrubby sheep!" As he spoke the words, the truth seemed to crawl over him. He looked sharply at me. By now I had taken both boots off the table and set down my whiskey glass. The crowd had moved in tight as a whore's corset, and I was worried. Nelson turned to the newcomer. "Tell me, then, who you think this man sitting here is."

This was the part I was not destined to enjoy.

"That man sitting there?" He started to laugh. "That's Las Cruces Charlie! He's been run out of every town in the territory—Tucson, Nogales, Tombstone, you name it." Then he curled his lip, rested his hand on his pistol, and looked around at the crowd. "And don't nobody lay a hand on him till I'm through with him." His steely gaze rested on me. "Get up and follow me."

I did.

He cut a wide swath to the batwings and escorted me to the hitchrack, with two hundred pair of eyes on me. "You, Charlie, you went by my name? That's a laugh! A real horse laugh! And you know what? I like a good joke, a joke like the one you pulled here. And you know what else? I'm gonna give you a twenty-minute head start on the honest ranchers of Five Pigs."

I just stood there, hornswoggled. He wasn't going to do what Deke Maginnis was famous for doing. I'd heard some ugly stories about him, like the rest of the town had—dragging Mexicans around, shooting the queues off Chinamen.

"You better fork your hoss and get moving, Charlie." He pulled out his watch, held it in his left hand, and laid his right hand on his widow-maker. "I'll hold 'em for twenty minutes. Recommend you go by way of the Little Sisters."

So, there I was, riding hell-for-leather across the scorched range, through what looked like a battlefield littered with burned and swollen cattle, toppled windmills, the charred remains of ranch houses and barns, and drifting flecks of ash everywhere. My horse was wheezing, and my nostrils were filled with the stuff, even with my kerchief up. The air cleared a mite as we pushed across Gila Flat, and below me I could see the honest ranchers, as Deke Maginnis called them, coming out of the burned plains and pounding after me. Thought I to myself, I'd have to be on my toes when I crossed trails with those sheepherders.

Then I was at the foot of the Little Sisters, and my horse was starting to get winded. I got off and walked him for a way, and I looked back to see the ranchers gaining ground on me. I put a foot in the stirrup, and as I swung my leg over the cantle, I told myself for the first time in two days, I sure have a knack for making a mess wherever I go. Then I thought of Deke Maginnis, and how hard he must be laughing back in the Silver Gila, and I smiled to think how nice it was to bring a little sunshine into the life of at least one fellow human.

ABOUT THE AUTHOR

John D. Nesbitt has pursued the western way of life since he first wore a black Stetson in his childhood, and for the past thirty-some years he has lived in the plains country of eastern Wyoming, where he enjoys camping, hiking, horseback riding, and hunting. As an author of more than forty books, Nesbitt also dedicates a great deal of time to reading, writing, and language study.

John has won wide recognition for his work, including two awards from the Wyoming State Historical Society (for fiction), two awards from Wyoming Writers for encouragement of other writers and service to the organization, two Wyoming Arts Council literary fellowships, four Will Rogers Medallion Awards, a Western Writers of America Spur finalist award for his novel *Raven Springs*, and the Spur award itself for his short story "At the End of the Orchard" and for his novels *Trouble at the Redstone* and *Stranger in Thunder Basin*.

PART FOUR

THE INFAMOUS BANDIT QUEENS BY GARY MCCARTHY

The Infamous Bandit Queens

Gary McCarthy

Copyright 2018, Gary McCarthy

Wolfpack Publishing
6032 Wheat Penny Avenue
Las Vegas, NV 89122

THE INFAMOUS BANDIT QUEENS

IN THE 1870'S, Belle Starr was outrageously described by a dime novelist in this way, *"Of all the women of the Cleopatra type, since the days of the Egyptian queen herself, the universe has produced none more remarkable than Belle Starr, the "Bandit Queen" more amorous than Mark Antony's mistress, more relentless than a Pharaoh's daughter; and braver than Joan of Arc."* This flowery tribute differs markedly from the descriptions that Belle applied to herself when she said, *"I regard myself as a woman who has seen much of life."* Belle might just as well have added, "hard" before the word "life."

Belle Starr was born Myra Belle Shirley in 1848 on her father's eight hundred acre farm near Cathage, Missouri. Little is known about her parents except that her father was reported to have been from an aristocratic Virginia family. This is partially supported by the fact that Belle received an excellent upbringing and education at a private academy where she studied Greek, Latin and Hebrew. But somewhere in her child-hood, sweet, innocent little Myra became tough and absolutely ruthless Belle. Part of her dramatic meta-morphosis can be attributed to the fact that Belle found herself embroiled in bloody times as guerrilla warfare erupted over the issue of whether or not Kansas was going to be admitted to the Union as a free or a slave state. Her brother was shot down and her father lost everything in the turmoil and moved his family to present day Dallas, Texas.

In 1866, the James and Younger brothers robbed their first bank in Liberty, Texas and fled south with six thousand dollars in cash and bonds. Cole Younger met the eighteen-year- old Belle and she fell wildly in love with him; a love that she would later proclaim never diminished although she took many lovers. After her passionate affair with Cole Younger, Belle gave birth to a daughter she named Pearl. It wasn't long at all before she was jilted by the handsome Cole Younger but Belle was now permanently hooked on the outlaw life. Within months, Belle took up with a man named Jim Reed, a noted bank and train robber. With the law close behind, the Reeds moved to California. But the California Gold Rush was long since over and the

Reeds found life out West difficult so they returned to central Texas where they began to rustle horses and cattle. There is some evidence to suggest that Belle and her man tortured an old Creek Indian until he revealed where he had hidden his lifetime savings. Whether or not this is true, it typifies the hard natures of Belle and Jim Reed who both gained notorious reputations. Enterprising dime novelists cashed in on that notoriety and Belle was soon known throughout our American West as, "The Bandit Queen."

Belle Starr, never considered especially physically attractive, gloried in her new celebrity. She dressed up in velvet gowns, plumed hats, white silk blouses and shiny black boots. When she galloped into town on her flashy black mare, "Venus," she was quite a spectacle with a pearl-handled Colt strapped around her hips. Belle's language was salty, to put it mildly and she made wonderful newspaper copy. Soon, legends began to sprout about all manner of exploits that she and her outlaw husband were involved in, most of them wildly fictionalized. That changed, however, when Jim Reed was gunned down in 1874 by a member of his own outlaw gang. Belle Starr left her daughter Pearl and infant son with her mother and set out to enhance her flamboyant reputation.

From 1875 to 1880, she was the undisputed leader of a band of horse and cattle thieves who plagued the country around the "The Nations" which as a huge patch of reservation land in eastern Oklahoma. An Indian named "Blue Duck" became her constant companion and lover until he was replaced by a tall, dignified Cherokee by the name of Sam Starr. Belle was twenty-eight; her new man was only a few years older. For awhile, the pair lived peaceably on Starr's small farm near the Canadian River. But times were hard and Belle soon tired of reservation living. Arrested for stealing horses, she and Sam were brought before the famous, "Hanging Judge" Isaac Parker. The pre-trial atmosphere was carnival-like. Belle Starr was besieged by newspaper reporters and she was not above lavishly embellishing her escapades as the "Bandit Queen." For perhaps the first and only time in his harsh and unbending career as a federal judge, Isaac Parker was lenient and Belle and her husband received only short prison sentences.

Both Belle and Sam Starr were model prisoners, but they certainly were not reformed. Sam was killed only a few years later by an Indian deputy whom he had shot and wounded in a drunken rage. Belle, once again a widow, soon took up with a young Creek Indian named Jim July. Like all her men, Jim had larceny in his heart and quickly got in trouble with the law. In 1889, Belle convinced Jim July that the government had no proof against him that would stand up in court so July agreed to surrender to the authorities. Belle accompanied him half way to Fort Smith, Arkansas where Judge Parker still presided. On February 3, 1899, just two days before her forty-first birthday, while riding home from a friend's house at Eufaula, Oklahoma, she was ambushed and shot dead. No one was ever arrested for the murder of Belle Starr and historians today still dispute who murdered the "Bandit Queen."

But the story is not quite over. Her daughter, Pearl, hired a stonecutter to carve an image of Belle's beloved mare, Venus, along with this epitaph; *"Shed not for her the bitter tear, nor give the heart to vain regret, this but the casket that lies here. The gem that fills it sparkles yet."*

Exactly ten years later, another Pearl whose last name was Hart teamed up with Joe Boot and robbed a stagecoach near Globe, Arizona. They reaped $431.00 and a place in history as having committed the very last stagecoach robbery in the West. Unfortunately, they got lost in the vast Mohave Desert trying to escape and almost died before a posse rescued them. Pearl was sentenced to a five-year prison sentence at the dreaded Yuma Territorial Prison. For several years after her parole, Pearl made a comfortable living off a lecture tour where she was regarded as a curiosity and celebrity. A short time later, Pearl vanished into historical obscurity, the last of the "Bandit Queens." We can only hope that she did not rob or shoot too many innocent people during the remainder of her mysterious life's journey.

A LOOK AT THE DERBY MAN BY GARY MCCARTHY

Darby Buckingham was an unlikely candidate for western frontier life. From his round-toed shoes to his derby hat, he was a man of culture, a creature of comfort, who liked his gourmet restaurants and expensive cigars. The short, stocky New Yorker made a fortune writing dime novels about the old west. Now he was out west to do some research for his next novel, little suspecting that he would be joining sheriff Zeb Cather in a manhunt for the ruthless Raton Brothers, learning firsthand about frontier justice and frontier heroism.

AVAILABLE NOW ON AMAZON

ABOUT THE AUTHOR

I have been writing American West historical and western novels for quite a few years now and have been fortunate enough to win a number of national writing awards for novels published by the biggest NYC publishing houses. My love of the West and its history runs deep and stems from the travels and the interesting places where I've lived. I have a B.S. degree in Animal Science from Cal Poly, Pomona and an M.S. Degree in Agricultural Economics from the University of Nevada, Reno and as a boy I grew up on horses and worked on several ranches during my summers in Idaho where I really began to appreciate ranching and big country. Later, while employed as an Economist in Carson City for the State of Nevada, I began to take adult education writing class under a wonderful Professor Emeritus named Dr. Paul Eldridge. He taught me how to tell a story and that creating memorable characters was always far more important and difficult than simply focusing on a plot.

I love researching my stories almost as much as I do

writing them and at the end of my historical novels, I always tell the reader what is real and what is not... when you can enlighten as well as entertain...it seems to me that is pretty special and I sure appreciate it from the authors I read.

I live in the small historic town of Williams, Arizona "Gateway to the Grand Canyon" and enjoy hiking and riding my buckskin Quarter horse, Sassafras; I blogged about my experience taking her to Monument Valley for a week of horse camping and riding. What a fantastic experience that was! I learned so much about the Dine "The People" ...the Navajo... so that I can write a really good novel about them someday just like I wrote about the Hualapai Indians "The People of the Tall Green Pines" who live along the rim of the Grand Canyon and whose story, RIVER THUNDER won a very prestigious national writing award.

If you love stories born of our great American West, I sure hope you'll give mine a try. Happy Trails!

PART FIVE

THE GUNFIGHTER'S GIFT
BY VONN MCKEE

The Gunfighter's Gift: A Western Short Story
Vonn McKee

© Copyright 2017 (as revised) Vonn McKee

Wolfpack Publishing
6032 Wheat Penny Avenue
Las Vegas, NV 89122

THE GUNFIGHTER'S GIFT

THE STRANGER RODE SLOWLY, like he'd been riding for a thousand miles. To my eyes, it seemed he just appeared from nothing, a sudden outline against the July afternoon sky. Old Jumper raised up from his sandy spot off the end of the porch and growled deep.

It was my sixteenth birthday. We'd just finished having pound cake, something we only had on special occasions. Ma stood holding three tin cups, still cool from the cider we drank. Daddy eased the front legs of his tipped-back chair to the porch boards. He shaded his eyes and squinted in the direction Jumper's nose was pointing.

When the visitor crossed Chugwater Creek, we could see he was of a thin build and wore a big light-colored Stetson that shaded his face. He rode a stocky pinto. Daddy stood then and folded his arms.

"Who is it, Henry?" Ma said, looking at him, then me. "Can you tell from here? Willie?" Daddy said nothing ... just stood there, frowning. I shrugged.

When the rider passed the row of Ma's hollyhocks at the edge of the yard, Jumper barked and started to run out but Daddy called him back. The man was older than I'd first thought, with a darkened weather-lined face. I remember thinking that, for his age, he rode straight in the saddle.

He eased down off the pinto like every joint in him was sore. Then he walked up within about ten feet of the porch and took off his hat. "Henry. Florence. You're looking well," he said.

I was bumfuzzled. I looked at Daddy and his face was red; his jaws were clenched and working. Ma just looked worried. The hair along Jumper's backbone was standing straight up but he stayed put, watching.

The man came up to the edge of the porch where I stood with my arm around a post. He looked right up at my face, reached into his shirt pocket and pulled out a blue box, kind of long and flat. He held it out to me. I can still picture him with those gray eyes looking into mine. Eyes that looked like they could be mean and hard if need be, but that day they were crinkled at the edges...maybe even a little teared up. I took the box from his hands and read the name written on it in silver..."Borsheim's," and underneath that in smaller letters, "Omaha."

"Happy sixteenth birthday, Wilhelmina," he said, his voice soft and rough at the same time.

Without even looking at Ma to see if it was all right or wondering how he knew my name, I took the top off the box and there was the first string of pearls I had ever seen. They looked like beautiful little full moons, creamy with swirls of pink and yellow and blue in the sunlight.

"I know you don't remember me, Skeeter," he said. "I haven't seen you since...goodness, since..."

"Since she was three years old," Daddy said. He didn't sound very happy to see the man.

The old man turned to Daddy. "Three years old. That's right. You always had a good memory for numbers, Henry."

"I remember a lot of things, not many that were good. So, what brings you here, Pap?"

Pap! I should have known. He was never discussed in our house but I'd seen a photograph of him on my grandma Ellen's bureau. He resembled my daddy, only really young...and smiling. I never saw that picture again after Grandma died. *Had he always called me Skeeter?*

"Aw, I guess I done what I come here for," said Pap.

"Wasn't sure I was gonna make it in time. Like to have missed the party, I see."

Daddy snorted. "Oh, you wouldn't miss a party now, would you?" I cringed when he talked with that tone. Pap kind of smiled and looked down at the dust. He nodded his head a little, like he'd been expecting the harsh reply.

"No, son. There was a time...a long time, in fact...I wouldn't have. I know it don't mean anything to you but I done quit all that." He put his hat back on and thumb-hooked his front belt loops. He looked like he had a lot to say but didn't know how to start. Finally, he said, "Well then. I'll just be going."

"You...you got some place you have to be, Pap?" It was Ma. She still held the cup handles on her fingers. Daddy shot her a hard look but she kept her eyes on the man standing in her yard.

"Well, naw. Not really, Florence. But that's all right. I need to get on along. Thank you, though. That's kind of you."

Like Ma, I got my nerve up too. "We got some cake left. I wished you'd have a piece with us," I said.

Daddy looked clammed up like he did sometimes when Ma and I outvoted him on something. "Pap, for goodness sake, you may as well stay the night," said Ma. "It's forty miles down to Cheyenne. And you don't need to be sleeping on the ground when you got kin right here."

Pap bit his lip, waiting for Daddy to say something, I guess. He just looked at Pap and waved his hand like he wasn't part of the decision.

"I'll stay in the barn. How about that?" said Pap. And he wouldn't hear of anything else, no matter how Ma fussed.

I caught up with him before he led the pinto inside the barn. I held the box from Borsheim's to my chest. "Pap! I just wanted to...well, I wanted to thank you for the necklace. Are they..." I was suddenly embarrassed. "Are they really real pearls?"

Pap grinned at my reddening face. "Yes, ma'am. Every one of 'em is a real pearl, Skeeter. Just like you."

* * *

Pap's night in the barn turned into weeks. He didn't ask to stay. Ma just kept insisting...and he kept refusing to sleep in the house. We could see that Pap was not in the best of health. Without the big Stetson, he looked kind of frail and bent. Funny how that all changed when he sat on a horse.

He and I took to riding together in the mornings after I'd fed the chickens and finished my other chores. Pap pitched in when he felt up to it, probably even when he didn't. Ma went on along like he had always been a part of the household but Daddy, well, he was another thing. He never had much to say when Pap was around. It made for some quiet meals.

Early one evening after supper, I went outside to feed Jumper the table scraps. Pap had hit the hay, I guess you could say. From inside the house, I heard Ma saying something in her "now listen here" voice although I couldn't understand the words. It wasn't long before Daddy jumped in with both feet and they were having a fine disagreement. I stayed outside where it was safe.

"You weren't there, Florence. You never saw him push my mother around, or box my ears, or trade the hog for a bottle of whiskey. You didn't hear whispering in the school yard that your pa was a hired gun..."

I took off for the hen house before I heard any more. I couldn't imagine old Pap doing any of those things. Well, maybe the gun part. He kept a Colt Equalizer hanging on a peg right by his hay bed and blankets. It sure looked like a serious piece of equipment. But to be mean to Grandma and Daddy...that didn't sound possible.

Chickens have always calmed me down when I was upset. They were already roosted and wondered what I was doing there, no doubt. I stroked the backs of a few hens. Their soft feathers and half-closed eyes did the trick, and I finally stopped shaking enough to go back to the house. Ma and Daddy were on the porch, calling for me.

* * *

"You know, I never have cared much for a spotted horse."

Pap and I were out riding. The grass was nearly up to our stirrups, tall enough to be cut for hay. I knew I'd be out here helping Daddy in a couple of days at most.

"What've you got against a spotted horse?" Pap said.

I looked his pinto over. "Well...I don't mean to offend. It just seems like the spots take away from the lines of the horse. You can't tell much about his cut with all that going on. Looks to me like you can hide a nice-looking horse under all those spots. Reckon you can hide an ugly one under them too." Just then, I felt like I had spoken a little too much of my mind.

"But I don't mean your horse," I added. "He's a fine one."

Pap laughed. "I ain't offended, Skeeter. Guess that settles it, though."

"Settles what?"

"Reckon I won't be leaving you my horse when I die."

Before I could answer, he dug in the spurs and that pinto took off like a racehorse. I jabbed at my Puck's sides and he jumped forward into a fast gallop but I knew we'd never catch up. When we topped the rise at the far south end of our farm, I could see Pap standing under a cottonwood, loosening the pinto's cinch strap. I got down and did the same for Puck.

I hadn't noticed until then that Pap was wearing his gun belt. The Colt's handle caught the sun. The wood was stained dark and shinier in places like it had been handled...quite a bit.

"You expecting trouble, Pap? Not much out here except coyotes and prairie dogs. The Cheyenne have been quiet of late."

Pap touched the holster and smiled. "Thought we'd drill a few pine cones or something. Never hurt a lass to learn to shoot."

I got a little knot in my stomach. Daddy kept a Winchester hanging on the wall...his "skunk killer," he called it...but I was forbidden to touch it.

He tied off the horses to a thick low-hanging limb of the cottonwood. Then he put his hands on his hips and surveyed the surrounding landscape, eventually nodding in the direction of a clump of twisted pines thirty yards off.

"Left side," he said. "Three of them." I spotted the branch with three cones spread like a chicken foot at the end, bobbing in the wind.

I never even saw Pap pull the gun out of the

holster. A loud blast filled the air, followed by a puff of sharp-smelling smoke. Puck reared up a little and tossed his head. The pinto was tugging mouthfuls of grass, like he was used to such goings-on. I could see that the middle pine cone was missing from the branch but the ones on each side were untouched.

While I watched, there were two more loud booms close together and the pine cones vanished one after the other. I looked at Pap and was surprised to see him crouched a little. The Colt was still smoking in his right hand and he held his left arm out to the side and bent at the elbow. His eyes were squinted hard. I'd never seen a real gunfighter in my life but I would have bet my string of pearls I was looking at one right then.

"Pap! You drilled them all right."

Next second he was smiling again, just like nothing had happened. He reloaded the empty chambers. "Why don't you have a go at it?" He held out the Colt. I took it in my hands, thinking it felt a lot heavier than it looked.

"But Daddy never lets me..." Pap ignored me and went on.

"Here...hold it this way, Skeeter. You ain't cradling a hen." He guided my fingers around the grip of the gun and touched my pointer finger. "Keep that one free for the trigger. Now, pull the hammer back with your thumb." I figured out that it took both my thumbs to get the hammer to click.

Pap pointed to a pine about halfway between us and the one he'd shot at. "There's a big clump of cones sticking out at the top. Look right down the barrel and put the sight under them. Then squeeze the trigger."

I tried to do just what he said. Next thing I knew, my ears were ringing from the shot and my arm felt like it was broken. I had no idea what I had hit, if anything. Most likely a piece of Wyoming sky.

Pap's voice sounded muffled. "Not too bad for a first shot. At least you missed the horses. Try it again. Maybe use your other hand too."

I held the Colt at arm's length and wrapped both hands around the grip. The pine cones swayed a little in the breeze but I tried to level the sight under the clump.

"When you get them in your sights, hold your breath just before you pull the trigger," Pap said. "Come on, Skeeter. *Draw a bead on the sumbitch.*"

I blushed hotly. I was not accustomed to such language. Nevertheless, I took a deep breath and focused with all I had on the tip of the gun sight. For just a second, it seemed like there was no sound and nothing else in the world except me and those pine cones. I squeezed on the trigger, slower and steadier this time. The shot did not startle me as before, since I was ready for it.

"That's my girl!" hollered Pap. I lowered the Colt and looked at the top of the pine. I saw only the splintered end of a branch...nary a pine cone.

We raced again on the way home. Pap let me win, I know he did. As the house came into view, I was thinking that there wasn't a happier girl in Chugwater Valley.

* * *

"What was all the shooting about?" Daddy was on the porch. He had what my Grandma Ellen used to call "a frown on his face like a wave on the ocean." I felt I should somehow take up for Pap.

"It was me, Daddy. I begged Pap to let me shoot at some pine cones. I even hit one."

"Reckon you forgot all about it not being allowed... handling a gun."

"I know you said I wasn't old enough. I thought maybe since I turned sixteen it would be all right. I'm sorry, Daddy. I should've asked you."

I could tell Pap was about to spill that it was his idea. "Maybe you could come with us next time," I said, hoping to cut Pap off and maybe cool Daddy's temper.

Daddy looked from me to Pap. "I don't have an interest in shooting. And I've a notion there are more useful things you could be doing. Why don't you go inside and help Ma for a bit?"

It worried me to leave them. But I said my *yes sirs* and went in the house. Ma was peeling potatoes for supper.

"Willie! Everything all right? I heard gunshots."

"Pap was showing me how to shoot a pistol." Over the fire hung a small kettle filled with water for the potatoes. I jostled the burning wood with a poker. "Have you ever shot a gun, Ma?" For some reason, I thought of Pap's words *draw a bead on the sumbitch* and it made me smile.

"Oh, no. Of course not. Not very seemly for young ladies, in my opinion." She shrugged. "I guess here in Indian country it might be a good thing to know." It seemed she made the last comment to herself more than me.

Just then, I heard Pap's voice outside, louder than I'd ever heard it. "...just spending time with my grand-daughter," he said.

"Well, ain't that a noble thing. It's a damn shame you never thought to do the same with your own son."

Ma and I looked at each other, then she dropped her eyes back to her potato peeling like she was embarrassed at overhearing the quarrel.

Daddy was wound up. "I'll thank you to not teach your gunfighting ways to Willie. Don't reckon she knows how much killing money you and that Colt have made. Hell, you probably don't even know..."

"There's plenty *you* don't know about that, Henry. I never shot any man that didn't need killing. It was done for reward money, not entertainment, and most times there was no gunplay involved. I'm done with it all anyhow."

The men were silent for a minute. Then Pap spoke again, calmer this time. "Henry...I know I was a no-account father to you. I didn't do right by your mother neither. I've lived with that day and night. Not until I lost everything I loved in this world to drinking whiskey did I lay it down...only it was too late. Thought I'd spend my last days with what family I got left. I see now that was a foolish notion. I'll be leaving in the morning, Henry. You were good to let me stay this long."

Pap must have gone to the barn. Daddy stayed on the porch and rolled a cigarette. I could smell the smoke from it. We had potatoes and cornbread for supper, just the three of us.

* * *

Just before dawn, a hard summer squall bore down on the farm. I was awakened by the rattle of thunder and a fierce wind whining around the corners of the house. Dust blew in through the door cracks. Then the rain came down in a loud rush and did not let up until midday. The south hay field would have to wait.

I figured that Pap wouldn't go anywhere in that weather but I couldn't be sure until the rain stopped. I walked, almost ran, to the barn, leaping puddles on the way. The sun had come out with a vengeance, and steam rose from the water-soaked ground. Pap was currying the pinto. His stuffed saddlebags lay just inside the barn door.

"Howdy, Skeeter," he said. "That was a toad strangler, eh? Thought the roof was gonna leave me a time or two."

"I kind of like storms," I said, "but Ma doesn't. She gets a lot of knitting done when there's a hard rain."

"Say, Skeeter..." Pap stopped brushing. "I decided I'd...I'd ride down to Cheyenne, maybe on over to the North Platte country, to visit some fellers I used to know. Most of them are old ranchers now. Like to see them all before they start getting hauled off boots first."

"I heard."

Pap looked uncomfortable. "You heard."

"Pap, I heard you and Daddy fussing yesterday. I... I wanted to say I'm sorry. If you hadn't been trying to teach me to shoot, none of this would have happened."

Pap hung the curry comb up on a nail and turned toward me. "Oh, Lord, Skeeter. None of it's your fault. This goes way back to when your daddy was a boy.

He's got a right to be sore with me. I wasn't much good to him, or your grandma."

"Well, I think he ought to forgive," I said. "That was a long time ago and things are different now. I don't want you to leave, Pap."

He lifted the Stetson and scratched his head. "Wilhelmina, you are a pearl, just like I said. It was worth everything to get to be with you for a time. But I don't think I ought to stay."

"At least wait a day or two. Chugwater Creek's got to be over the willows from all the rain."

"That's so, I reckon."

"I'll talk to Daddy," I said boldly. Pap didn't answer, just nodded.

But I didn't have to talk to Daddy. He walked in the barn just then. "Creek's way up," he said. "Be foolish to try a crossing. I'd wait a few days." That was all he said.

* * *

The next day was Sunday. I only had one dress I hadn't outgrown and I'd worn it to church the last four times. We would sell hogs in the fall and the money would bring calico for new dresses, maybe even a new pair of lace-up shoes. Fluffing up the limp ruffles on my sleeves, that seemed a long way off. I'd been begging Ma to let me wear my pearl necklace to church but she said it would look proud.

"Please, Ma," I beseeched. "If I don't wear them to church, then where? The town dance is more than two months away. I'm aching to show them to Myra Lundberg."

She threw up her hands. "Oh, all right then, Willie. Go ahead and wear them. But don't be surprised if you get some down-the-nose looks."

I was so happy I war-whooped just like a Cheyenne. Ma helped me with the clasp and, looking at myself in Daddy's shaving mirror, I smoothed my collar under the necklace. *Real pearls.* Myra would be so envious, but in a best friend sort of way.

Looking in the little mirror, it was curious to me how much I had changed of late. My frizzy blonde hair had turned a few shades darker and settled down into waves. My face wasn't round and kiddish anymore. I put my hand on my cheek and felt the smooth flatness of it. When I turned away, I caught Ma staring at me, her eyes soft and a little sad.

"You're a pretty girl, Wilhelmina." I didn't know what I should say.

Daddy drove the buckboard close to the porch and Ma and I climbed on. We squeezed into our places on the seat beside him. The wagon lurched and bounced all the way to church but I did my best to sit tall and elegant like a queen.

* * *

Ma was right. Valeria Hobart about twisted her head off looking back at me during church. I could tell she was dying to know how I came by a string of pearls. She was pretty enough but her mouth always turned down and her nose wrinkled up like she smelled something sour. Then she whispered something to her mother and Mrs. Hobart looked back with that same look on her face. The resemblance was very strong among the Hobart women.

Myra Lundberg loved the story of Pap riding out of nowhere on my birthday and handing me a jewelry box. She made me tell it to her three more times before I headed home.

When we pulled up to the barn, Pap was laboring over a small fire he'd built in the open yard. He was turning a rabbit on a spit and, from the smell, it was nearly done.

"Sunday dinner's on me today, folks." He grinned as he rubbed butter over the meat.

Ma smiled and joined him, holding her skirts back from the smoke. "I have applesauce to go along with it...and cornbread from last night," she said. I was relieved when Daddy didn't mention anything about hunting on Sunday.

I went inside to help Ma get things on the table. Through the open door, I kept an eye on Daddy. He unhitched the mule and put him in the outside pen to enjoy a little grass and sunshine. Pap was pulling on a rabbit leg to test its tenderness. Daddy joined him at the fire.

They started talking. It didn't appear to be a quarrel, just looked like two menfolk visiting. Daddy held a big skillet under the rabbit while Pap eased it off the spit.

"Willie, set the plates and then go pick a couple of hollyhocks for the table," said Ma. She smoothed a cut linen tablecloth on our rough old pine table and straightened the scalloped corners. It had been a wedding gift and I'd only seen her use it a few times.

I carefully arranged our plates and silverware and hurried out to pick the flowers, almost bumping into Pap. The roasted rabbit was sizzling in the skillet he held. "Whoa there, lassie. You nearly upset my apple cart!" He was in fine spirits.

I broke off two hollyhock stalks covered with fluffy blossoms, the palest pink with purple at the centers. Ma held them out to admire them before she put them in a small crock jar. "Grandma Ellen brought those seeds all the way from east Texas," she said, then looked at Pap quickly. I saw her bite her lip.

"Then we better put them over here by me," said Pap, still smiling. I confess that I teared up when he said that. I so wished Grandma Ellen could have been at our table. Those beautiful hollyhocks would have to take her place.

Daddy said grace. Pap passed out portions of the browned meat. He told us a couple of stories about when Daddy was a kid...the time he climbed a tree and couldn't get down. He had to spend the night up there and all the neighbors showed up to look for him. Then the time Daddy and his cousin Pete decided to white-wash the milk cow. Ma and I laughed and laughed. Even Daddy smiled, more than once. It was the best meal I could remember ever having.

* * *

When the dishes were washed and the tablecloth was folded and put away, Ma and I decided to rest on the porch before changing out of the Sunday clothes we still wore. Pap appeared at the barn door. He led the pinto, saddled and loaded, as if for a long trip. I felt a knot in my stomach. When he got to the porch, he tied the horse to the post.

"Creek's down a good bit from yesterday," he said. I knew it was so. We had driven along Chugwater Creek on our way to church. "Reckon with some luck I'll be sleeping in Nebraska tonight. Ain't but thirty miles."

"That's about right," said Daddy. I jumped a little. I didn't know how long he'd been standing in the door-way. "Long time 'til sundown this time of year. You oughta make it that far." I wanted to beg Pap to stay but I didn't dare cross Daddy. He didn't seem to be in favor of it.

"Well, I'm going up on the hill to visit a lady before I go," said Pap. He nodded toward our family graveyard between the house and the creek. "Like to come along, Skeeter?" I looked at Daddy to see if he objected but he said nothing.

Ma said, "Hold on, Pap. Take these hollyhocks with you. I've been meaning to take flowers up there."

Pap stepped up on the porch and, much to her surprise, kissed Ma on the cheek. "You are a good, good woman, Florence." She looked flustered and twisted her hands in her apron. Pap and I headed for the grave-yard. I carried the jar of flowers. I noticed he had his Colt strapped on.

The little cemetery was surrounded by a row of thick cedars that Daddy had planted back when my twin brothers had died. I had been only six years old. The boys, Matthew and Mark, were tiny from birth and both got pneumonia at about a year old. They died ten days apart. Grandma Ellen joined them in eternal rest when I was twelve. I placed the flowers at her marker.

Pap leaned over and traced her name on the carved wooden headstone. "You had no business marrying the likes of me, Ellen Denby. But I'm thankful to my God above that you did. I knew I wasn't good enough for you. Partly why I left like I did. I was a sorry drunk back then."

He straightened up and wiped sweat from his face. "By the time I decided to act like a man, it was too late." I didn't know if he was talking to me or Grandma Ellen.

"Skeeter..." Pap turned to me and took my hands between his. "I want you to remember what I'm telling you. I was a scoundrel on many counts. But hear me out on this. I made my living as a bounty hunter, bringing in some mighty lowdown characters over the years. Most of 'em I brought in alive. I got paid honest reward money for what I done."

"I believe you, Pap," I said. "I just know you wouldn't have killed anybody out of meanness."

"Well, some would disagree. Listen..." He pulled a slip of paper from his shirt pocket, the same one he'd taken my box of pearls from. Only a month ago? He pressed the paper into my palm and closed my fingers around it.

"Here's the name of a bank in Denver where I keep my account. They have orders from me to send a draft to Henry. Ought to arrive within the month. Skeeter, it's clean money and I want you to make sure your daddy gets it. If he don't want it, then tell him to put it in a bank in your name. It's...it's near twelve thousand dollars."

"But Pap..." I said. "you can't give away all your money."

Pap laughed. "I never said I was giving it all away. I got enough for beans and cigars."

There was a sudden great crash of branches behind us and we turned to see a big sorrel horse burst through the cedars only five yards away. The rider was a heavy man with a bristling beard. The horse charged between Pap and me and, before I could react, the man reached down and grabbed my arm...slinging me up into the saddle in front of him. He pulled the horse hard and it reared to face Pap, who was standing, legs apart, with the Equalizer pointed right at us.

"Well, Dub Denby! Reckon you're surprised to see me again," the big man shouted from behind my head. His meaty arm was wrapped around me, pinning my elbows at my sides. "Didn't know you had company up here. Makes things more interesting, don't you think?" He laughed and I smelled tobacco and sour liquor and a rotten odor that made me feel sick.

"You're here to see me, Sid. Let her go," said Pap. His gray eyes were like stones.

"Ha! That'd be tender-hearted, wouldn't it? You wasn't so obliging to my brother Rolf. You plugged him just about...here." With his free hand, the man named

Sid pressed the muzzle of a pistol in the flesh just below my collarbone, and the pearl necklace I'd forgotten to take off.

"Your brother was already holding a gun on me when I drew," answered Pap. "She's unarmed and got no part in this. You and Rolf made your way. You knew it was going to end with a bullet or a jailer's key."

"Reckon you got a purty thick wad for hauling in the Gothard Brothers. Damn shame one of us only brought half price, being dead and all. As for me, they's not many jails that can hold me for long. I been hunting you for six months now. And I get to do the killing this time, Dub."

Sid Gothard slid the barrel up to my temple. "Maybe I'll shoot this little gal too. Might be a fine idea for you to drop that Colt about now." I wanted to signal Pap not to give up his pistol but I didn't dare move. I mouthed "no." Thought maybe I could figure out a way to give him a clear shot at this smelly man behind me.

Pap lowered his gun and bent down to lay it gently on the ground out in front of him. Then he took a step backward. "Now...let her go, Sid."

The next minute passed slow, like a dream. Sid straightened his gun arm all at once and aimed at Pap. I threw all my weight to the side, broke free and tumbled off the horse. I heard a shot and got to my hands and knees to see Pap crouched like he was that day under the cottonwood. But there was no gun in his hand. He looked right at me real calm, then he collapsed.

I scrambled for the Colt...still on the ground between us. I must have spooked the horse because he threw his head up and danced backward a few steps... just long enough for me to get my hands on the grip. I knew Sid would be aiming for me next time. When I swung the pistol around, I saw that it was true.

Hold your breath...squeeze! I heard the shot, but somehow, I knew it had come a split second before I pulled the trigger. Was I hit?

Sid Gothard had a quick look of surprise on his face, then he tilted to one side and slid, falling heavily to the ground.

I heard a footstep. *Pap?* I spun around, the Colt still clasped in both my hands. In the gap of the cedars that Sid had ridden through, stood Daddy...holding his Winchester rifle, a curl of smoke rising from the barrel.

We both ran to Pap. He was bleeding from his upper chest, near the very spot Sid had threatened to shoot me. "Daddy, do something for him!" I was on the edge of crying. He leaned over and listened to Pap's chest. Then he stripped off his own shirt, rolled it into a ball and pressed it on the wound.

I saw Pap wince a little. "He's alive!"

"Let's get his head up. Here...can you move around and let him rest on your lap?" Ma ran into the graveyard. Her cheeks were bright red and her hair combs were slipping out.

"Oh, my dear Lord!" she said. "Henry, Willie...are you hurt? Pap? Oh, good heavens, he's shot!"

"We're both fine, Florence. Pap has taken a bullet... and that fellow over there probably took two." Pap moved his hand to his chest, then opened his eyes. He appeared to be in dreadful pain.

"Henry...Florence. He..." Pap whispered.

"Don't try to talk, Pap," I said. He put his hand on my arm, leaving a smear of blood.

"I...never meant for trouble...to follow me here," he said. "Forgive me..."

"Don't worry over that," said Ma. "He said he was your old business partner. I told him you were up here. I am so very sorry, Pap. I should have..." Her voice quivered as she stroked his cheek.

"There was something about him didn't look right," said Daddy. I felt a rush of gratefulness toward him. *What if he hadn't come when he did?*

"Henry...I might not..." Pap was struggling to speak. "I need...to tell you..."

"Hush, hush..." Ma whispered. "Can we try to get him to the house?" Daddy was inspecting the entry wound and reached behind the shoulder, feeling for something with his fingers. He nodded. I was relieved that, if Pap was going to die, it wouldn't be there in the graveyard.

The old man would not give up on talking. "Henry...all for you...all these years...saved up. There's money. Skeeter knows where..." *The paper!* I must have dropped it when Sid grabbed me. Without getting up, I made a quick look around and finally spied the crumpled slip resting near Grandma Ellen's grave.

"Hang on, Pap," said Daddy. "Don't get in a hurry to cash in your chips. You ain't going anywhere...least not today. Looks like your biggest gripe is gonna be a bum shoulder." Daddy gently picked him up and I realized how slight the old man was. "Grab hold of that horse, Willie," he called back to me. "We'll figure out what to do with that dung heap later." I reckoned he meant Sid Gothard.

As we walked down the hill...Daddy carrying Pap with the Colt laid on his belly, me leading the sorrel and Ma toting the Winchester...Pap looked up at Daddy and said, "That was a fine shot, Henry."

Daddy grinned, more light-hearted than I'd seen him in years. "Well, I just drew a bead on the sumbitch...just like you told me, Pap."

A LOOK AT THE SONGBIRD OF SEVILLE BY VONN MCKEE

The citizens of Sugar Creek had never seen anything quite like Señorita Rosaline De Caro of Seville, Spain - a world-renowned soprano on her way to a performance in Denver. What is initially a brief stopover while the stagecoach is repaired gets significantly more complicated for everyone involved, especially the sheriff, due to a very unexpected shooting...

The Songbird of Seville was a 2015 WWA Spur Award finalist for Best Short Fiction.

AVAILABLE NOW ON AMAZON KINDLE

ABOUT THE AUTHOR

Vonn McKee brings deep storytelling to the western genre, rich with emotion and vivid pictures of a beautiful but unforgiving land and the hardy, spirited people who settled it. She often weaves real-life historical events into her writing, adding realism and intimacy to the characters and storylines.

Vonn broke into the western writing scene in 2014 with The Songbird of Seville, a short story that was chosen as a Spur Award finalist by Western Writers of America. That same year, The Gunfighter's Gift was named a finalist for the Peacemaker Award for short fiction by Western Fictioneers.

She grew up in the Red River Valley of Louisiana, where her mother's family settled in the mid 1800s, and spent summers at the northwestern Minnesota ranch where her father grew up, picking up details about horses, cattle, and agriculture. Inspired by seeing her grandfather stretched out on a sofa reading Zane Grey novels (some of which were passed down to her), she owned a complete ZG set herself by age eighteen.

Vonn loved hearing her grandmother relate stories of her childhood spent on the Dakota prairies, which were similar to Laura Ingalls Wilder's accounts in the Little House series of books.

Vonn McKee now calls Tennessee home. She has reviewed books for Roundup and True West magazines and, although her first love is writing short fiction, she is working on a historical novel series.

PART SIX

A PROMISE BROKEN, A
PROMISE KEPT BY
V.J. ROSE

A Promise Broken, A Promise Kept: A Western Short Story

V.J. Rose

© Copyright 2018 (as revised) V.J. Rose

Wolfpack Publishing
6032 Wheat Penny Avenue
Las Vegas, NV 89122

A PROMISE BROKEN, A PROMISE KEPT

A CRIMINAL LAWYER never forgets his first murder case. I have practiced law for thirty-five years, except for a brief period of insanity when I served as governor, but nothing I ever experienced compared to my first case.

I had studied law for two years with my uncle but had yet to appear in court on my own. My uncle had achieved a certain amount of fame as a trial lawyer in West Texas. When four dust-covered, leathery-faced ranchers appeared in the office after three days of hard riding and requested his services, it was not deemed as unusual.

The case they put before him, however, was. A woman rancher stood accused of shooting the son of her bitterest enemy after the young man had been heard boasting to several people he intended to "run her off her land" for good. That the defendant was a woman made my uncle's eyebrows rise immediately. Prostitutes were often put on trial for murder in frontier Texas—other seemingly decent women, never. But the woman rancher had incurred the wrath of a wealthy and powerful neighbor, the boy's father, by refusing to sell her small ranch to him.

The evidence was circumstantial, but strong. Every Sunday for the past twenty years, rain or shine, she had attended church, but that Sunday she had stayed home. That afternoon the victim was found not half a mile from her house, shot between the eyes. Her reputation of hitting a target over a hundred and fifty yards away with a Winchester was so well known that it had kept many a foolish man from going where he was not wanted. There was not a man, woman, or child in the county who could shoot that well.

"My God," my uncle exclaimed, rapping his cane on the floor as he sat with his foot propped up on a stool. "Tell me something good. What about her reputation? Is she married, a widow?"

What the ranchers explained at least worked in her favor. Twenty years previously, her husband had left on a cattle drive, promising to return. He had not, and she had spent those years taking care of her elderly father-in-law and the ranch with the help of her brother. The father-in-law had long since passed away, the brother more recently. Since then she had struggled on alone, much admired for her character and tenaciousness.

And then they came to the crux of the matter. The ranch she owned was at the headwaters of a river. And water was all important in West Texas. Whoever controlled the river controlled the land for hundreds of miles. If she was convicted, the wealthy neighbor would swallow her ranch, eventually putting all the smaller ranchers around him out of business. That she be cleared was imperative to their livelihood, hence, their desperation.

My uncle remained silent for several moments. Finally, he pointed to his foot. "My gout will not allow me to make this trip," he told the men. Directing his cane at me, he said, "My nephew will go instead."

I tried not to let my surprise show. The men looked at me with harsh, questioning eyes. "Is he any good?" one of them asked.

"He's not as good as I am," my uncle said briskly, "But he is the best you can get. Go to the hotel, get cleaned up and eat. In the morning, he'll join you, and you can leave."

They filed out of the room reluctantly. As soon as the door shut, I turned to my uncle.

"You can't win this," he said abruptly, reaching for a cigar. "The wealthy neighbor will buy off the jury and half the town. But no one will really expect you to. It's a way for you to start a name for yourself without too much damage to your reputation."

My first look at the defendant was a shock. At thirty-seven most women of the time looked old and worn out. Katie Blackwell retained much of her youthful prettiness. Blonde hair wrapped around her head like a crown; her wide blue eyes had a habit of staring intently, and the full pink lips of her mouth trembled slightly.

She had little to tell me. She said she had not killed the boy and had no idea who did. She had not gone to church that day because she felt ill. Even with so little to go on, I felt buoyant after leaving her. Surely no jury in the world would convict such a woman of quiet dignity and beauty, despite the fact she could shoot a squirrel's eye out at a hundred yards.

I was a curiosity in town, and true to the reputation of the West, the men there were of few words, and I had to drag what information I could from them. My uncle had often commented wryly that if our clients said they were innocent, they were. However, any aspirations of victory I had began to melt as it soon became apparent that everyone in town believed her guilty.

No one knew how the rumor got started that Katie's husband had not wanted to come home. His partner had come back with a terse story explaining he had disappeared, and other than that, he had little to say. He had shared the money made from selling the cattle, however, and it had kept the young woman afloat until her brother arrived to help her. Years later, on his deathbed, the partner had sent for her, but died before she could reach him. She had been courted by many men and had almost said yes a time or two, but always backed out. She had a reputation for being kind, but stubborn.

It was that stubbornness that made me begin to doubt her innocence. She had protected her property against all comers for twenty years, and the evidence seemed stacked against her.

Any remaining hopes I had of an acquittal disappeared in the courtroom. A special prosecutor had been brought in, and he smiled at me with long teeth that slyly said, "I will eat you alive." The judge's teeth were almost gone, the ones left stained with tobacco juice that he spit incessantly while staring at me in disapproval. The crowds of sweaty people made the courtroom look and smell like bleachers for a circus.

It was the father of the murdered young man who ground away the last optimistic thought I had, however. He sat behind the prosecutor, jowls thrusting, his large bulging eyes staring with a single-minded purpose at every person in sight, and that look told of his burning intent to see Katie Blackwell swing for the death of his son.

Much to the disgust of the judge and the prosecutor, I took all day to pick a jury. I tried to remember every instruction my uncle ever gave me, but it was plain I was hesitant, unsure, and out of my depth. The look of silent despair in the eyes of my client deepened with every tick of the courthouse clock.

That night, I sat alone in the hotel dining room, crumbling my bread, unable to eat more than a few bites, keenly aware that every eye there was watching me. One old man sat apart, and he caught my attention because he was different from the rest. He had a neatly trimmed white beard, white hair combed back, and he wore a black suit with a black string tie. He looked out of place in a room full of boots and bandannas, but his presence was such that no one thought to deride him. His clear blue eyes gazed at me objectively and without embarrassment. Feeling as if I had already lost the case in the minds of everyone in the room, I rose and left.

It wasn't much later that a knock sounded at my door. I opened it and there stood the old gentleman in the black suit. He stuck out his hand.

"Rufus King, at your service, sir," he said.

There was nothing I could do but invite him in. He

pointed at one of the chairs and asked, "May I?" I nodded and he sat down.

"You were wise to take your time picking a jury," he said. "It may or may not do your client any good. But despite inciting the ire of your colleagues, it raised the public's opinion of you considerably."

Back then, I lacked the intuition born of experience I have now, but even so, I had an immediate flash of perception that night. "You are an attorney yourself, sir?" I asked.

"Yes, yes sir, I am," he replied, and we set off on a conversation about law that has never again given me so much pleasure. He had an encyclopedic knowledge combined with a rare gift of insight that thrilled me then and does to this day when I recall it. He not only knew every landmark Texas Supreme Court decision, he explained them so a raw young country lawyer could understand every facet and ramification.

After over an hour of talk that passed as quickly as a few seconds, he put his hands together and said, "Now tell me about the case against this woman."

I found myself spilling every detail, and in the end, blurting, "My God, sir, would you consider taking over and letting me assist you? I fear I will get that poor creature hanged."

"That will be for her to decide," he said and rose.

"I'll be back at dawn, and we can discuss it with her together."

He left, and I felt a great load lift from my shoulders, although a niggling thought told me the outcome had been his objective the entire evening.

The next morning, I introduced Rufus to Katie and stood nearby while they sat across from one another at a coffee-stained table in the jailhouse. I hope never again to see the depths of emotion in a woman's eyes such as what I witnessed that morning as she stared at the man who might conceivably free her. It was almost too much to bear, but Rufus gazed at her evenly. "I think I can get you out of this dilemma, Mrs. Blackwell," he said. "Will you allow me to represent you? I promise to do everything I can."

Never removing her eyes from his, she finally nodded.

"Good," he said, and proceeded in the same calm reassuring tone. "We can do this one of two ways. You can trust me to get you acquitted, or we can find someone to say they shot the young man."

I immediately objected. "Sir! You can't possibly mean...."

Rufus held up a hand to stop me, never taking his eyes from Katie. I might as well have not been present; she didn't acknowledge me but continued to look intently at Rufus. Finally she nodded. "I trust you," she said in a voice so low I had to strain to hear.

He took her hands and caressed them gently. "Now tell me about this business of church. Why didn't you go?"

Under his kind probing, the real story came out. The preacher had visited her the day before.

"When I turned to the stove to reach for the coffeepot," she said in a halting voice, "he came up behind me and cupped my breasts in his hands." She covered her lips with her hand and lowered eyes for the first time. "I asked him to leave, and he did. But I had wanted him to continue. I..," and she began to weep soft tears. "I was lonely and afraid, and I wanted very much to lean against him." She looked up at Rufus and tried to control herself. "His wife is my friend. I was so ashamed for the way I felt."

"My dear woman," Rufus said. "Even Christ was tempted."

She calmed and continued. "I started out for church, but just before I got there, I couldn't bring myself to go on. I turned the buggy around and came home. I thought I heard shots along the way, but I can't be certain." She had seen no one.

When we left the jail, Rufus informed me he would meet me in the courtroom, and he disappeared without another word. He made it back in time to be standing by my side when the judge walked in, but just barely.

The prosecutor gave a long and flowery opening statement, and I could see by the avid faces around me that his histrionics satiated their craving for the sensational and just as dramatically impressed them. Rufus's statement was to the point and disappointingly short. "This woman is innocent, gentlemen, and I intend to prove she was unjustly accused."

It continued that way all day. The prosecution called witness after witness. We listened as five men described seeing the victim late Saturday night in a bar drinking and ranting repeatedly that he intended to get Mrs. Blackwell's place by force if necessary. Six witnesses described watching the defendant shoot a rifle with incredible accuracy. Three church deacons got on the stand and swore that in all the time Mrs. Blackwell had been attending church, she had never before missed a Sunday.

Rufus remained silent throughout, never objecting and almost appearing pleased. The crowd in the courthouse felt cheated and disgruntled. He did not impress them or me, and I began to wonder if the lawyer I talked to the night before had just been a wishful dream on my part.

When the prosecution rested its case, we adjourned for the day. Rufus leaned to Katie and gave her hand a reassuring squeeze. "Don't worry," he whispered. "We have let them fire all their ammunition; now we will open our guns."

At the restaurant that night, Rufus paid little attention to the barbed looks thrown his way. As I looked around, I wondered. Was it my imagination? Were seeds of sympathy being sown for Katie Blackwell for having two such sorry attorneys? I didn't question Rufus; he disappeared and left me alone with my doubts.

The next morning, he recalled the sheriff. After the sheriff had hoisted his fat belly in the witness chair and positioned himself, Rufus began.

"Sheriff, you told the court yesterday of finding the victim with a bullet hole right between the eyes, didn't you?"

"That's right," the sheriff said with a smirk. "Smack dab between the eyes."

Rufus walked carelessly around the courtroom, as if nothing of importance was going on. "Would you tell the jury where you found the body?"

The sheriff grinned. "Sure, I'll tell it again. Right up yonder on Mustang Ridge."

Rufus turned to face the jury. "Yes, but exactly where on Mustang Ridge? On the road? By the side on the road? Fifty, a hundred yards away from the road?"

The smug complacence left the sheriff's face to be replaced by wariness.

"Sheriff? Would you answer the question, please?" Rufus said, turning around. "Exactly where did you find the body?"

The sheriff licked his lips. His eyes began to search for the man who had originally reported the death and found him sitting forlornly hemmed in by the four ranchers who hired me. "About a hundred yards from the road," the sheriff finally managed to murmur.

"Will you speak up, please? The jury didn't hear you."

Looking like he had swallowed a snake, he repeated it louder.

"And whose property does that belong to, that stretch by the road?" Rufus innocently asked.

The sheriff looked at Katie and swallowed. "The defendant," he said. And a little louder to ward off another reprimand, he added, "Katie Blackwell."

Although the tension in the courtroom was building to almost unbearable heights, Rufus again wandered around the courtroom, unconcerned. "Mrs. Blackwell keeps her property fenced, doesn't she, Sheriff?" he finally asked.

I took a breath. The whole courtroom became as tense as tightly strung wire.

The sheriff nodded miserably. "Yes," he said

shortly. Sweat stains were beginning to appear under his arms.

Rufus spun around, looking like a much younger man. "And what condition was that fence when you arrived, Sheriff?"

The victim's father almost exploded into murderous rage. He half rose and gave the prosecutor a vicious jab in the back. He jumped up. "Objection, your honor, the condition of Mrs. Blackwell's fences have no bearing on this case."

The judge spit into a nearby spittoon, and said, "Overruled. Answer the question, Quintus."

"They were cut," the sheriff said, giving in completely to misery. "The wires were cut."

"No further questions, your honor," Rufus said.

The prosecutor tried to undo the damage by redirecting questions and adding, "So he really was just barely on Mrs. Blackwell's property?" But the harm had been done.

Although the courtroom remained silent, the sheriff's testimony produced a sensation and massive shift in public opinion. The sheriff, looking haggard and ill got down from the stand, and as he walked by the victim's father, he gave the old man a look that said, "I couldn't help it." The old man looked at him as if he were a spineless worm, and it was then I knew how deeply they had been in collusion with one another.

What could be passed off as a death by the side of the road on Mustang Ridge was now something entirely different. A few jury members exchanged glances with one another.

"I call as my next witness," Rufus said, "the Reverend Bagby Simms."

The Reverend was a middle-aged man, stout and virile, and it did not surprise me that a woman might be tempted by his ruggedly handsome features. What he was being forced to do was clearly distasteful to him, and he did not try to hide his disdain for Rufus.

"Reverend Simms," Rufus said. "You visited Mrs. Blackwell on the Saturday before the murder, did you not?"

"Yes," he said curtly.

"And did something happen during that visit to upset Mrs. Blackwell?"

The Reverend sifted in the chair and answered with a short "yes."

"And will you explain what happened during your visit to upset Mrs. Blackwell."

The Reverend lifted his chin. "I tripped and fell. I tripped and fell against Mrs. Blackwell."

"And when you were trying to right yourself, where did you accidentally touch Mrs. Blackwell?"

If looks could kill, Rufus would have been sitting on a cloud playing the harp. "I accidentally touched

Mrs. Blackwell's bosom," the reverend said through gritted teeth.

"And then what happened?" Rufus asked.

"I apologized and left."

I looked around the courtroom. Not one adult believed there was anything accidental about that quick feel. A woman sat with her face rigid, clinching her teeth so tightly together, her jaws looked locked. I knew it was his wife. And she knew, and I knew, and everyone in the courtroom knew that Reverend Simms's career as a minister was over in West Texas.

"Now Reverend," Rufus said, "isn't it possible, that a woman with fine feelings might be embarrassed by what happened, so embarrassed she couldn't face attending church the next day?"

"Objection, your honor," the prosecutor said, "We haven't established that Mrs. Blackwell has these finer feelings."

"I did not say the defendant's name your honor," Rufus countered. "I merely asked the Reverend with his vast experience as a minister, might a woman feel that way."

"Answer the question, Simms," the judge growled. "And you," he said pointing to Rufus, "don't get tricky."

Rufus quickly said, "Yes, your honor," and Simms again answered as if saying the words were killing him, "Yes, she might."

The prosecutor did not cross-examine, and Rufus called his next witness.

"Maritza Gonzales," he said.

A gasp rose throughout the courtroom. I tried to look wise and knowing, but had no idea who this woman could be. The prosecutor jumped up and shouted, "Your honor! I object! This hollowed court is no place for a Mexican peasant woman to appear!" Nevertheless, a plump little brown woman waddled her way to the front. A deep scar ran across one side of her forehead.

"Your honor," Rufus interjected. "I cite McDavid v. Sanchez, eighteen...."

The judge cut him off. "Don't start that balderdash in here." However, he glared around the courtroom and said, "There is no law that says a Mexican woman can't testify in court."

She had never slowed down on her way to the witness stand anyway. After being sworn in, she sat down with lips tight, scanning the courtroom and daring anyone to stop her from talking. The victim's father had turned purple with rage in the meantime.

"Miss Gonzales," Rufus said. "Would you tell the court what your former occupation was?"

"I was housekeeper to him for twenty years after his wife die," she said, pointing an accusing finger.

"Let the record show that the witness is pointing to

the victim's father," Rufus said. "Now Miss Gonzales, you became more than a housekeeper, didn't you?"

"Yes!" she said defiantly. "I had his children, but he would never marry me. He always wanted her and her ranch!" she spat and pointed at Katie.

"Mrs. Blackwell?"

Her yes was drowned out by the prosecution's objections. The judge told him to shut up and sit down.

"Miss Gonzales," Rufus said. "What happened seven years after Mrs. Blackwell's husband disappeared?"

"He started gossiping that he heard the man hadn't wanted to come back. He didn't know nothing! He wanted her to be disgusted and have her husband declared dead! And then he would move in and try to take over."

"Objection, your honor! This is hearsay!"

The judge leaned toward her. "Did he tell you this?"

"I heard him talking about it. I am not deaf."

The judge looked at Rufus. "Continue."

"Miss Gonzales, how did Mrs. Blackwell respond to the victim and his father? Did she bring over neighborly gifts of food or ask advice on ranching?"

"No! She distrusted them!"

"Objection!"

"Sustained. Leave the 'no' and scratch out the rest."

"I'll rephrase the question, your honor," Rufus said. "Did Mrs. Blackwell ever come to their ranch and threaten the victim and his father?"

"No! Never!"

"When you knew the victim's father had been to her ranch, what was he like when he returned?"

"He was furious! The last time, he come home and give me this scar!" she said, pointing to her head. "My son, he say, 'Mama, let's leave here. This man, he may be my father, but he is no good.' So we leave."

"So the victim would see his father coming home from Mrs. Blackwell's ranch in a foul and vindictive mood," Rufus said.

"Yes!"

"No further questions your honor."

The prosecutor conferred with the father. He stood up and said, "Madam, what were you doing when you got that scar?"

Miss Gonzales sneered. "I was hitting him with a frying pan."

A ripple of laughter went through the courtroom, but the prosecutor ignored it. "Isn't it true madam," he said in loud voice, "that you were insanely jealous of the defendant, so jealous that you would be willing to lie on the witness stand to hurt your ex-lover? Isn't that so?"

"Yes! But I am not lying now!" Maritza Gonzales screamed. "He hates her for rejecting him and would do anything to hurt her and get her property."

During that speech, the prosecutor had been trying in vain to get his voice heard above her tirade. He finally yelled, "That is enough!" To which she promptly began to curse him in Spanish words that I dare not repeat here for fear of burning in everlasting hell.

It took some minutes to get her off the stand. When things calmed, Rufus rose and said in a voice that rang throughout the courtroom, "I call Katie Blackwell to the stand."

This was the moment everyone had been waiting for. Once on the stand, Katie never took her eyes off Rufus.

"Mrs. Blackwell," he began kindly. "Much has been made about your expert marksmanship in this courtroom. Tell us, who taught you to shoot?"

"My husband," she replied.

"And did you ask your husband to teach you how to shoot?"

"No," she said, "I didn't want to learn. He said I needed to know."

"You don't tote around a rifle just for the fun of it then? You don't carry your gun to church for example?"

"No."

"That's fine," Rufus said. "Now, was your husband a good shot?"

"Your honor," the prosecutor objected. "Really, what difference does it make if a man who has been dead for twenty years was a good shot or not?"

"Your honor," Rufus said. "I can show you where I'm going with this in just a minute."

"I already know where you are going. Proceed."

"Well, Mrs. Blackwell?"

She nodded. "Yes, he was better than me."

"How many brothers did your husband have, Mrs. Blackwell?"

"Your honor, please!"

"Shut up!" the judge said, abandoning protocol.

Rufus nodded at Katie, and she continued. "He had thirteen brothers."

Rufus walked around the courtroom. "Thirteen brothers!" he exclaimed. "Are they all good shots? Are they all capable of shooting a man between the eyes from a great distance?"

Katie answered a breathless "yes."

"Do they live in Texas?" he asked.

"Yes, except one lives in Louisiana."

"Did your husband think his family had a monopoly on fine shooting?" Rufus asked.

At first she didn't seem to understand the question. As she stared at Rufus, a remembrance dawned into her eyes, and she almost smiled. "No, he didn't. He used to tell me about the crack shots from Tennessee he made friends with during the war who were better than he was."

Rufus smiled and facing the courtroom, he said, "Yes, the Southern soldiers were superior marksmen, weren't they?"

My estimation of him went up even more. West Texas was largely settled by poor crackers and Southern gentry who had lost everything in the war. It was also a sly dig at the prosecutor. Someone had recently spread the rumor his mother was a Yankee.

"So you know of, and have heard of, lots of men who are even better with a rifle than you are, isn't that so, Mrs. Blackwell?"

She nodded. "Yes."

Rufus drew close to her, almost touching her. He stared at her intently, and in a quiet voice, he asked, "Mrs. Blackwell, did you stay home from church on purpose to wait for someone you thought was going to try to take your ranch from you?"

"No, sir," she said, shaking her head.

"Did you lie in wait near Mustang Ridge, waiting for the victim so you could put a stop to his threats?"

"No sir."

Rufus nodded. "Did you shoot this young man, Mrs. Blackwell?"

"No sir."

"No further questions, your honor."

If Rufus had appeared a meek lamb at the beginning of the trial for refusing to object to the prosecutor's questions, he now roared objections like a lion at every query put forth. After fifteen minutes of getting nowhere, the prosecutor finally quit.

In summing up, the prosecutor did his best, but he was a defeated man the minute it came out in a Texas court that the victim had cut a fence and was on Katie's property. Rufus gave a brilliant summation resulting with nary a dry eye in the courtroom. He stressed over and over the many men, especially Katie's in-laws, who were capable of shooting a man between the eyes at long range. The members of the jury who had been bought off by the victim's father began to look uncomfortable, thinking it was perhaps better to have one known enemy rather than a dozen unknown ones. In five minutes, they brought back a verdict of "not guilty."

Amidst the cheers of congratulations, Rufus whispered that we would hustle Katie out as if she were going back to the jail to get her things, but instead take her to a horse and buggy waiting by a side door. The ruse worked, and as we stood alone by the buggy, I had to ask him.

"Where did you learn law like that?"

"In prison," he said with a smile. "I made the mistake of killing a man in self defense in another state. The warden there, a former attorney, took a shine to me and let me study his books." He paused and looked at Katie. "When I left home, I promised my beautiful young bride I would come back with riches. Since I thought I was going to be incarcerated forever, I decided it would be better for her and my family to believe I was dead." He looked back at me. "I made such a good attorney; the other prisoners requested I represent them in court, and the warden allowed it. I got the governor's nephew off, and he granted me a pardon."

"You mean?" I gulped, standing there like a gawky teenager that I was not far from being. He helped Katie into the wagon, but before he could get in, I pulled him aside.

"Wait a minute. How did you know she was innocent? How did you know where the body was found?"

Rufus looked at me and grinned. "Because I did it, junior. I killed him."

"But you would have let your wife hang?!" I asked, flabbergasted.

"Of course not. And I asked her right in front of

you what she wanted me to do." He smiled again at Katie. "She forgave my broken promise that day and accepted a new one."

They drove away arm in arm while I stood watching with my mouth open. There was no use of ever accusing him of murder—he was too much for me. Nonetheless, nineteen years later my silence paid off when Rufus reluctantly gave me his charming eighteen-year-old daughter as a bride. I think Katie, however, was happy to have me as a son-in-law. ###

TESTIMONY

BY V.J. ROSE

When his old friend Rocky shows up at Jack's West Texas ranch to spend the summer, he brings along his sexy granddaughter, Toni. Thrilled at first, Jack begins to have doubts. Toni is hiding something even as she freely admits doing whatever it takes to keep Rocky and herself afloat. Jack finds himself so happy he doesn't care if he's being used; besides, he's hiding secrets of his own.

AVAILABLE NOW ON AMAZON.

ABOUT THE AUTHOR

V.J. Rose is the author of several novels set in the New and Old West. She was a 2014 Western Writers of America Spur Finalist for her short fiction story about an attorney on his first murder case, "A Promise Broken, A Promise Kept."

Born in a small Texas town, she grew up listening to tales of shootings and lynchings, while in the meantime devouring her grandmother's romances and her mother's mysteries. She couldn't deny a lifelong love of writing, and throwing herself into it, earned a degree in journalism in her fifties, attending universities first in East Texas and later in West Texas.

She lives with her son, Dan, two cats, and a dog in Central Texas, ten miles from where she grew up.

THANK YOU

Thank you for taking the time to read the *Western Short Story Showcase, Volume One.* If you enjoyed it, please consider telling your friends or posting a short review. Word of mouth is an author's best friend and much appreciated.

Thank you.

Wolfpack Publishing

Made in the USA
Monee, IL
29 January 2021